my name is mitch

Shelagh Lynne Supeene

ORCA BOOK PUBLISHERS

National Library of Canada Cataloguing in Publication Data
Supeene, Shelagh Lynne

My name is Mitch / Shelagh Lynne Supeene.

ISBN 1-55143-255-2

I. Title.

PS8587.U59M92 2003   jC813'.6   C2003-910707-8

PZ7.S9585My 2003

First published in the United States, 2003

Library of Congress Control Number: 2003106160

Summary: Mitch is tired of being called Midget and being picked on by the class bully, and he is tired of his mother's refusal to tell him anything about his father, whom she calls The Creep.

Orca Book Publishers gratefully acknowledges the support for its publishing programs provided by the following agencies: the Government of Canada through the Book Publishing Industry Development Program (BPIDP), the Canada Council for the Arts, and the British Columbia Arts Council.

Cover design: Christine Toller
Cover illustration: Helen Flook
Printed and bound in Canada

05 04 03 • 5 4 3 2 1

IN CANADA:
Orca Book Publishers
1030 North Park Street
Victoria, BC Canada
V8T 1C6

IN THE UNITED STATES:
Orca Book Publishers
PO Box 468
Custer, WA USA
98240-0468

To the memory of my mother, Margaret Geekie Supeene, 1923-2000, who heard about Mitch although she didn't live to read his story; and to my family, Tom Slee, Jamie Supeene and Simon Slee, with love.

SLS

1.

My name is Mitch MacLeod. On the first day of school I can tell that it's going to be a bad year. The first people I see are Philip Mahavolich and Siobhan McAllister (a.k.a. Shove-on a.k.a. Chevy). As soon as I walk into the classroom Philip points at me and yells, "Hey, Midget-brain, the kindergarten is down the hall." Everyone looks, naturally, including any new kids I might have had a chance with.

Chevy chips in, "Here, little boy, I'll take you to Mrs. Granoff." She holds out her hand. You'd never know that over the summer we were practically friends. She totally towers over me, but I ignore her. The good thing about Chevy — the only good thing — is that she has the attention span of a flea. She catches sight of Zoë and Nicky, her sidekicks, and takes off.

I walk over to a big desk in the back and dump my new backpack on it. The backpack is black with red trim and lots of compartments. It is the best one I've ever had. My old blue one, which I've had for years, had holes everywhere. Every time I had to take money to school, like every Tuesday for pizza, I lost it, unless my mother taped it to a big piece of paper. Then of course Philip was merciless. He'd untape the four quarters or the loonie and say it was for my own good. "Can't let a little kid like you have money — you might put it in your mouth and choke on it!" Big guffaws from Richard and the rest of the big-head no-brain crowd.

Lucky for me, new prey walks in before Philip can get going. Maria's clothes are always either too big or too small, and they're never what everyone else wears. *And* she wears glasses. Philip hates people who wear glasses. I should know.

As soon as Maria walks by Philip, he jumps back like he's been burnt. "Yuck, cooties! Pass them on!"

But just as he touches the guy next to him, this big voice booms, "Philip Mahavolich, you know that game is banned. No recess for you today."

Right away Philip starts acting all innocent. As he's whipping around to see who's talking to him he's already saying in this dumb so-innocent voice, "Sorry, sir, I'm new, sir, I didn't know!"

Sir! He actually says, Sir!

Then he sees the teacher. It isn't a sir. It's a woman! And does she look mad. You should see Philip's face. He's got his mouth open to say something else, and when he sees her he just stands there, forgetting to close it.

The teacher's face gets red. She tells us to take our seats. Then she hisses to Philip, "You're already in trouble. Lying will only make it worse."

Her name is Ms. Murphy. She substituted at the end of grade five a couple of times; that's why she looks familiar. She gets right into math as soon as attendance and announcements are over. Long division. First she asks Philip to solve a problem on the board and he does okay. He usually does. "Very good, Philip," she says, and he swaggers back to his seat. Then she asks me, and she gets me to stay up for a few questions while she reminds people of the steps. Math is a snap for me, so I don't mind. Then it's recess.

Recess is good. A bunch of us play frozen tag. I'm feeling so good I even ask this new kid if he wants to play. He's standing under the tree holding a Game Boy, but he isn't playing, he's watching us. He says okay. I don't even tag him although I could have. He runs really slowly. He *lumbers*, in fact, like you imagine Frankenstein would, if he tried to run. When he's It, no one is in any danger. He would have been It for the rest of recess — for the rest of the week! — if I didn't let him tag me. Then I catch Jake Pfohl right away, and Jake always goes after Nicky, so the new kid isn't tagged again.

Back in the classroom Ms. Murphy is moving the desks. Before recess they were in three long rows facing the windows. Now they're in a big horseshoe. It takes awhile to find our desks. When everyone is sitting down, she says, "Okay, let's make sure everyone has a desk that fits him or her. Whose desk is too small?" Three kids stand up, including Philip.

"Who has a big desk but doesn't need it?"

I sit up very straight, and a little forward, too, so my toes touch the floor. I am *not* going to give up this desk. I never get a big desk, and I never get to sit in the back, either. Well, now there isn't any real back, but I want the big roomy desk, anyway.

Ms. Murphy looks around. I do too. It's obvious that there are only two big desks in the whole room. Most are middle-sized and a couple are really small, like for grade two kids. Would you believe Philip has one of those? He looks ridiculous. He's the size of a grade niner, for Pete's sake. He definitely needs one of the middle-sized ones, which Nicky really doesn't need. She's pretty small. She could go in the little desk.

I realize Ms. Murphy is talking. She says impatiently, "Mitch, are you listening? Trade with Philip, please, let's not waste any more time over this."

Just my luck! I get one of the tiny grade two desks! Naturally, Philip rubs it in. "If the Midget can't go to the kindergarten, the kindergarten will come to the Midget," he says.

It looks like this year is going to be just like last year. I hate being the shortest in the class! But hey, things can always get worse, right? And they do, because here comes reading.

Everyone talks while the assignment is handed out. We have to read two pages of small type and answer questions about it. Ms. Murphy seems surprised at how much everyone talks, and she keeps after people until they quiet down, but by then it's too late. My concentration is shot. When it's time to hand our work in I haven't answered a single question. I decide not to hand in my paper. On the way to wash my hands for lunch I throw it in the wastebasket.

2.

When I get home, Grandma's just getting back too, with some shopping. She teaches English at high school, and she usually gets home before I do.

"How was the first day of school, dear?" she asks. She starts unpacking stuff. It's just about all yarn, with a package of socks for me. Grandma crochets. Whenever she sees this certain type of yarn on sale she stocks up. Today she has bought two packages of brown, two of mauve, and two of white. I hope she doesn't mean the colors to go together, because it would look sickening.

Grandma is nice. When I don't answer her about school, she doesn't ask again. Instead, she tries to talk me into putting some plants in my room. Mum and I live in the upstairs apartment in Grandma's house. She says the eastern light would be perfect for her heart-leaf philodendron, and if she could move it to my room there'd be more space in her living room for the dracaenas and spider plants when they come in for the winter.

I'm firm, though. I know if I let one single leaf into my room, it'll be no time before my room is completely taken over. Like *Day of the Triffids*, which Dan read to me last year, where there are these monster plants that turn out to be from outer space, and they can think and move around and attack people. The philodendron is practically a triffid already. Or a giant squid. It is HUGE, and growing from three dozen places. Grandma says, "Maybe you'd rather have the fern, dear." No! Not the fern! Her fern is the size of a Volkswagen! Before Grandma can suggest anything else, Mum comes home.

"Whew!" she says as she kicks off her shoes. She does this every day. "The last customer was a no-show. She was going to have a perm too. Forty bucks right out the window. At least I get out early. Hey, buddy, how are you? Give me a big kiss."

She hugs me and kisses my cheek. Reaches for some grapes on the table.

Grandma says, "Why don't you and Mitch have supper here tonight, Tiffany? Dad's working late."

Mum shakes her head, which is pink. Her hair stands up like a brush, and this weekend she dyed it pink with a purple stripe. She's a hairdresser so she changes her hair quite often. She cuts mine too, but I won't let her dye it. She's working on me to try green, at least a streak. To match my eyes, she says. It wouldn't, though. It would end up being neon green or poster paint green, I'll bet. You've got to be a Richard or Chevy to get away with that.

She says, "Dan's taking us out for pizza to celebrate Mitch's first day of school."

Well, I like pizza but it *so* won't be a celebration. More like a wake. The first day of school is like a funeral for summer vacation. Last night I made up a cartoon story about it to cheer myself up:

"Here lies This Summer. This Summer will be remembered for the two weeks' camping with Mum and Dan. Dan got the itch and broke out in huge, itchy, red lumps. They were so itchy he couldn't bear to wear any clothes but his bathing suit, even when it got cold. Then he'd jump up and down beside the campfire to keep warm. The people at the next camp-site took one look at this maniac and got scared. They packed up all of a sudden and left in the dark. Mum and Mitch laughed themselves silly.

"This Summer Mitch spent a week at a cottage with Uncle Brandon. The women in the next cottage taught Mitch how to paddle a canoe. They came out to give him a lesson whenever Uncle Brandon appeared, and even when Mitch could paddle fine, they kept offering more lessons until Uncle Brandon invited them for a drink. Then they agreed that Uncle Brandon was right: Mitch could paddle okay on his own. They were all so busy agreeing on this that it took awhile for them to notice Mitch had capsized! Uncle Brandon spent the rest of the week making that up to him. They went to the waterslide, ate chips, played mini-golf. And no neighbor women.

"This Summer Mitch went to the Ex with Auntie Chris and they got separated. Mitch told Security that he was only eight years old, so he got to drink two Cokes and eat all the chips he wanted. By the time Auntie Chris found him he felt too queasy to go on any more rides, so she had to go on the roller coaster by herself.

"This Summer there were trips to the beach with Grandma and Ms. McAllister and Chevy, who spends the whole school year as a troll but who becomes an ordinary human as soon as school ends. Mitch and Chevy took their usual summer break from being enemies. They swam, played Nintendo, and spied on Chevy's sisters and their boyfriends. When they giggled too much Chevy's sisters heard them. She and Mitch ran like the wind.

"This Summer was fun, but it is gone. Rest in peace."

I drew a big cross on the last page and wrote "RIP" on it.

I like to make these things up, like about Summer having a funeral, and make a cartoon story out of it. I don't try to make the people like real people, they're more stick figures. Like Mum is a stick figure with a brush cut and a triangle for a skirt.

When Dan saw the picture of himself jumping up and down to keep warm, he didn't even notice the big, red, itchy bumps, which actually were hard to do on stick-arms. I draw him as a small "b" with arms and legs. All he saw was the big bump for his stomach. I put little marks to show it was jiggling. He got very huffy, said it was rude to exaggerate. I was ready to argue. His big stomach did so jiggle when he jumped up and down. I should know; it was right in front of me. But Mum frowned and shook her head.

She said, "Cartoonists always pick one feature to exaggerate, Dan. Mitch didn't mean to hurt your feelings." So I let it go.

Dan is my mum's boyfriend. She's known him for years, almost since I was a baby, but he hasn't been her boyfriend the whole time. Dan is a lot older than Mum, but most grown-ups are. She had me when she was only sixteen.

She and Dan would like to live together, but Mum doesn't want to move me away from Grandma because she works late quite often, and Dan can't move in with us because Grandpa would have conniptions.

Grandpa is the only person in my family that I don't get along with. I never put him in my cartoon stories, but if I did he'd be something hard — a rock or a nail. He is so hard-hearted that if he needed a heart transplant the donor would have to be a petrified mummy, or a big bronze statue. Even his eyes are hard. When he looks at you, you feel nailed and small.

Grandpa is often angry at Mum and me.

Mum says it is because he thought she shouldn't have had me until she was older, and married. That was eleven years ago, though, and he's still angry. Once when he was going on about it Mum said, "Try not to let him get to you, Mitch. He's ignorant. The only thing I regret about having you is I wish I could have waited ten years. Then you'd have had a mum with an education, like Auntie Chris and Uncle Brandon." Those are Mum's sister and brother. Auntie Chris is a lawyer, and Uncle Brandon is a university teacher.

It is true that Mum is the worst-educated person in her family. She didn't finish high school; she just went to hairdressing school. But she says that maybe it's just as well she didn't go to university because she really didn't like high school. She was glad to quit when she had me, really.

Maybe there's a gene for not liking school and I got mine from her. But what about reading? Mum reads all the time and so does Grandma and even Grandpa, when he's not watching the game.

The thing is, sometimes I can read and sometimes I can't. Like if Dan says, "What's on TV tonight, Mitch?" — no problem. I read the TV guide's listings and even the articles. The same with the captions on the pictures in the book about stars that Dan gave me, even when they have lots of hard words. Longer things are harder, though. Like whole chapter books. I don't read those myself.

And in school I can hardly ever read anything when the teacher asks me to. It's like I freeze. I can't think. The words won't talk to me. Sometimes, though, in silent reading I'll get a whole story read. That's if everyone is quiet. Grade four was the best. Ms. Richardson had the quietest, best classroom. I did quite well in silent reading in her class. No reading aloud, though. Tests were no good, either. I'd freeze even in her class when it was a test. She couldn't understand that so she did some special things to check my reading and I did fine — I did great! Because it was her, and she really liked me, and her room was always quiet. She's old. She must be Grandma's age, which is fifty-three. Ms. Richardson says she's an old-fashioned teacher. I liked her, though.

But last year with Miss Terpstra, reading was worse than ever. Everyone thinks it's pretty dumb not to be able to read except Mum. She figures I'll read when I really want to.

I really want to now, though.

Maybe I got my reading gene from The Creep. The Creep is what my mother calls my father. If I did, that's the only thing I did get from him. He was sixteen too, when I was born, but he didn't have anything to do with Mum or me. I don't even know his real name. He's never even seen me. It would be pretty unfair if the only thing he gave me is not being able to read. But I've noticed quite often things *are* unfair.

3.

Before Dan comes Mum changes out of her work smock into jeans and a shirt. She makes me wash my hands, but I don't have to change my clothes. Dan has changed. He has to. He's a mechanic so his work overalls are always greasy. He's a really good mechanic. He just got a raise so he wouldn't take another job.

As soon as we're in the car Mum reaches for the radio dial. The Beatles are singing, "I'll Follow the Sun" and she cuts them off mid-word. Nickelback blasts out on the new station. Mum sits back and says, like she has a hundred times before, "Dan, you are not old enough for the 'oldies' station." He reaches for the volume control and turns it down. "I like this song too," he says, "What do you think, Mitch? What do you like?"

I like a lot of things. I like songs on MuchMusic and MuchMoreMusic, both. I keep it secret who I *really* like, especially from Dan, who totally teases me. I'd never hear the end of things like "Mitch has a girl friend. She just has to wait a few years for him to grow up." Really unfunny, but he would say he was joking. And he'd think so too. He doesn't mean any harm.

Anyway, I'm taking no chances. I say, "I like Savage Garden."

Dan and Mum both go, "Who?"

"Backstreet Boys," I say instead, and they nod wisely. They've both heard of the Backstreet Boys.

When we get back from having pizza Grandma is out front, talking to some of the neighbors. She is wearing her jogging clothes, but it doesn't look like she's run yet. One of the people she is talking to is her best friend Ms. McAllister, who is also Chevy's mother. Grandma and Ms. McAllister went to school together, and they're always looking at me and exclaiming. Grandma goes, "Just think, Kathy, we weren't much older than Mitch and Siobhan when we met." (Siobhan is only known as Chevy at school where no one could pronounce her name.) Ms. McAllister goes, "Amazing, Susan. Remember, Jocelyn Ewasik?" And away they go with the same old two or three stories.

Now Grandma calls to us, "We're going to have a street dance!" She sounds excited. "First an outdoor buffet, then Kathy's girls are going to play. We're just thinking about when it should be." Chevy's sisters, Mairead and Sinéad, are in this band that everyone thinks is so great.

Mum and Dan *love* the idea of a street dance. I hate to admit it but my mother takes dancing lessons for fun, and so does Dan. I just know they are going to embarrass me unless I can somehow thwart this plan. So I say, "Grandma, maybe that's not such a good idea. Just think who might be attracted to a street dance."

Everyone looks at me.

"Who?" asks Grandma.

"Bikers!" I say. "They love to crash parties. And while everyone's outside, burglars will have a field day in people's houses! A big obvious street party is just an invitation to crime!"

Grandma says, "You worry too much, Mitch." And she goes back to planning with Ms. McAllister. They decide on the last Saturday of September, and are well into details of food and chairs. I start fooling around with the basketball.

Grandpa comes home, grunts at everyone, and goes straight in to watch the game on TV. It's too bad we don't get along. He's the only person in our house besides me who likes to play chess, but he only plays with Uncle Brandon. I go watch TV awhile with him, but I get this sinking feeling being alone with him. He doesn't talk to me, and even when I turn to look at him, he stares straight ahead, so I go up to bed.

The star book Dan gave me is beside the bed, so I look through it for awhile before I go to sleep.

As soon as I get to school the next day Ms. Murphy calls me up and asks where my reading assignment is. In a situation like this, my motto is, "When in doubt, lie." I say, "Oh, I handed it in, Ms. Murphy. My answers were a bit long so I had to use an extra piece of paper."

Then she moves her hand off a piece of paper on her desk. It's all creased like it was crumpled up and someone smoothed it out again.

"I found this in the wastebasket. The name has been erased, but if you look closely, you can still read it: Mitchell B. MacLeod. Why didn't you answer any of the questions, Mitch?"

I don't say anything. I don't know what *to* say. Sometimes when I look at a word it sits there on the page and talks to me loud and clear. Like with the TV guide at home. But at school usually all the words sort of talk at once and I can't hear any of them.

Ms. Murphy says I have to go see Ms. Petrillo, the special ed. teacher, right now. It seems about a mile from her desk to the door. Everyone stares while I walk, and walk, and walk. My face feels so hot it must be beet red. Philip calls, "Hey, you finally realized you're in the wrong class, Midget? Are you going to the kindergarten or the *junior* kindergarten?"

Ms. Murphy snaps at Philip that he will miss recess again. He looks mad. Also surprised. No wonder. Last year Miss Terpstra yelled all the time, but she never actually punished anyone.

Ms. Petrillo is short and round and somehow she seems to move quickly. She is probably the friendliest teacher in the school, without being loud and jolly. I hate loud and jolly. Some grown-ups sort of bawl at the kids when they are being friendly, like they are on stage and have to be heard in the last row. It makes me want to disappear, but that kind usually waits for an answer.

Ms. Petrillo talks at a normal volume and

seems just normally friendly, which is how it should be, right? Why should she act like I'm her best friend when she doesn't know me? Anyway, she isn't doing anything to make me nervous, but boy, I am nervous anyway.

I am there until recess. She tries to get me to read to her. I can't hear a single word, but she doesn't get impatient. She just tries other things. She shows me pictures and asks about them. She reads to me and gets me to answer more questions, and she gets me to write words for her. It's a disaster anyway. There's a class standing in the hall, waiting to go to gym, and the noise is all I can think about. I can't read at all. Nothing. My nose hurts like I might cry, but I pinch it hard and wipe the water from my cheeks, and I'm okay. She says not to worry, we'll work on it every morning until it comes. She means this to make me feel better, but my stomach feels like it has a big stone in it. That's all I need. As well as being the smallest and not being able to read, now I'm a "Special Ed" too.

The stone is still there at lunch recess. I watch the new kid play with his Game Boy. I wish I was allowed to bring mine to school. That way I wouldn't have to face anyone.

After lunch, we have to write a funny poem. It is quite fun. Ms. Murphy makes everyone be quiet — by now everyone has noticed how freely she cancels recess — and I get a good idea right away so there's lots of time to do the actual writing. Rhyming is hard, but I get it to work and I'm pretty pleased with it.

After awhile we have to read our poems to the class. The new boy goes first. I can hardly hear him because Chevy and her henchwomen get to whispering right in my ear. Chevy is on my left, and Nicky and Zoë are behind me.

His name is Daniel and he's written about his first karate class. It sounds pretty good, what I can catch of it, which isn't much. Zoë is giggling too loudly. When Daniel's finished, Ms. Murphy tells her she's missing recess tomorrow and the henchwomen all shut up, finally.

Then Ms. Murphy calls on me!

My poem won't sit still. It's moving on the page or something, first one word is clear, then another, but all out of order. Chevy puts up her hand and offers to read MY poem! And Ms. Murphy says, "Well, Mitch, who's going to read it?" I stare at the page for ages, but it won't work and I have to let Chevy.

This is my poem:

My Grandmother's Plant

My grandmother loves her plant.
Its leaves are shiny green.
She thinks it's like a baby, she thinks
it's just so sweet.
She doesn't know behind her back that
plant grows claws and teeth.

My grandmother loves her plant.
Its leaves are shaped like hearts.
She thinks it's like a vegetable, she
doesn't know it's smart.
It's got a knife all sharpened and is just
about to carve.

It took me ages to come up with the last two
lines. My first idea of a rhyme for "hearts" was
funny but too rude for school! Anyway, Chevy
reads it okay. When she finishes, she says,
"That's good, Midget!" She sounds surprised.
Actually, everyone seems to like it. They ask a
few questions and I get talking about triffids,
which gets everyone even more interested. Then
Chevy says, "You actually read this book,

Midget?" and there's a big, open, gaping *loud* silence. Finally I say, "Someone read it to me." After that, I don't enjoy the discussion as much.

I don't pay that much attention when the next kids read their poems. Then it's indoor recess because of the rain and I don't feel like doing much, so I just sit at my desk. The latest changing around of desks has put Daniel next to me. I figure he's one of the kids from this new subdivision that's being built out east. Whenever a new subdivision is being built, all the kids come here until they get their own school. Then they brag about the rubber floor in the new school's gym, and all the computer rooms, and leave us to our antique school when they move on. Then we get more kids from some other new subdivision until they get *their* new school.

It's better not to make friends with the subdivision kids because they don't stay. It can't hurt to just talk to one, though. Daniel has red hair and freckles and he's quite small, not much taller than I am. He's busy holding his Game Boy under his desk and working it like fury. Suddenly he says, "Stupid thing!" and turns it off.

"What were you playing?" I ask. He's got

5.

As you can tell, I am very particular about my friends. There are good reasons for this. The main one starts with "J." Joey was my best friend from grade three to grade five. Then the Meadowcroft School was built, and that's where he is now, I guess. He got to go see it with all the other bus kids last June, and they couldn't stop talking about how new and great it is. Computers for every room. Air conditioning!

We were going to keep in touch over the summer, and I called him, but he couldn't come over and I couldn't go there, either. Mum doesn't have a car. Also, she said I should only have friends over when she's home because it's not fair to Grandma. But she works a lot. Anyway, I haven't seen Joey since June. I never did see him at our houses, but at school we were a team. School is easier to take if you are on a team. Especially certain parts of school, like Philip's mouth and Chevy's gang.

The street party is set for the end of September. By then, I have got the hang of avoiding Chevy and her henchwomen. They don't look for me; they don't even notice me unless I get in their way. Philip is a different story. I would say Philip is getting himself quite a reputation at school, and not just with me.

For example, he doesn't even bother to bring lunch anymore. He just picks and chooses from everyone else's. He makes some excuse to go to the cloakroom, and at lunch a bunch of people are missing things. He doesn't bother with healthy things like carrots and fruit. He goes straight for chips and chocolate bars. If you have an egg salad sandwich, he'll leave it. If you have cheese, he might take it.

It doesn't even bother him when people see their sandwich boxes on his desk. He just says in this surprised voice, "Gee, however did my sandwich get in Daniel's box? Here's your box, Daniel."

One day he goes too far. He takes Chevy's chips. You've heard of the Cookie Monster.

Well, Chevy is a Chip Monster. She loves chips more than anything, even chocolate. So she goes rooting through her knapsack and when she can't find her chips she stands very still until everyone is looking at her. Then her eyes get narrow and mean-looking, and she's looking right at Philip.

He's sitting there with enough loot on his desk it's like he's had his own Halloween. He looks at her and leans his chair back on two legs, really casual. He reaches for one of the bags of chips and starts to open it. While he's been staring at Chevy, Zoë and Nicky have come up behind him and are leaning over him. Suddenly Philip notices them, and he sits forward with a thump.

Chevy stalks over and sticks out her hand. "Give me those chips," she snarls. Philip is still trying to look casual, but at the same time he's taking quick looks all around. There's no way out. He's surrounded. "These are mine," he says, but his voice is lacking a certain something. Chevy snatches the bag from his hand. She bends over and looks him in the eye. "Don't ever steal from me or my friends again or you'll be sorry, *Fill-up*." She whips back to her desk and she and the henchwomen laugh while they eat the chips. What a girl! She's magnificent! Just for a minute I am filled with admiration, then I remember she's no friend of mine.

But it is *great* to see Philip taken care of. Until he decides to get revenge. It happens during art. When Philip walks by my desk he knocks over the red paint. It spills right onto Chevy's picture! Chevy isn't here, so I try to clean it up while Philip says in this despairing voice, "Midget, Midget, can't you be careful? You've just ruined poor Chevy's painting." When Chevy comes back from the washroom, she sees me rubbing paint all over her picture. Quick as a wink she grabs the blue paint and dumps it all over *my* picture. I've just spent like an hour getting Smaug's wings right and now they are buried under a blue lake. My picture is completely ruined.

On the way home Chevy hisses, "Midget, you're toast. I don't care if my mum and your grandma *are* best friends, you are history. *Ancient* history."

So that is where things stand the night of the street party. It's a Saturday and for once Mum isn't working. She goes shopping with Grandma in the morning and in the afternoon she bakes cheesecake and apple pie while she listens to the radio turned up loud. Downstairs, Grandma has potatoes in the oven and beans in the Crock Pot, which smell delicious, and she is making a bunch of different salads. She's listening to the radio, too, on Dan's "oldies" station. Grandpa is out in the driveway setting up the barbecue. He's listening to the game on *his* radio. I'm running every which way, taking things out to the picnic table in the front yard and getting Grandpa his tongs and stuff. Everywhere I go it's a different radio station. Weird.

Then Dan comes with the hot dog buns and a case of Coke (my favorite!). We're unpacking things and putting the drinks into the fridge when he drops the bombshell. He invited his boss and his family. Dan's boss just happens to be Philip's father!

I already know Chevy will be coming, although they don't live on our street any more than Philip's family. Philip lives at least a kilometer away! The garage is just around the corner, but they don't *live* in the garage! Mum and Grandma don't care. "The more the merrier, as long as they remember it's potluck," Mum says. Dan says Philip's father is bringing steaks. Mum says she expects he'll find somewhere to cook them.

Suddenly, while they are talking about Philip's father, I get what Chevy called Philip. Philip's father's garage is called "Philip's Garage," because his name is Philip too. And on TV his ad has this goofy spiel between Mr. Mahavolich and a customer and then big letters spell, "Fill up at Philip's." "Fill-up": that's what Chevy called him. Of course, she's no one to talk about names, with a name that sounds like "Shove-on."

Grandpa has the barbecue going. It's an old-fashioned one with coals that you have to start hours ahead of time. He's standing out there with Mr. Sloan from across the street. Mr. Sloan has brought his barbecue over to our driveway to listen to the game. What game? *I* don't know. There's always *some* game on and Grandpa doesn't seem to be particular, he'll listen to anything. Mum and Grandma and Dan come and sit in the front yard too, and call hi to a few other neighbors when they come out.

Just as Grandpa's putting our burgers and veggie dogs on the grill, up drives this big gray van, honking its horn. It's Mr. Mahavolich. I've seen him at the garage. He jumps out and opens the side door. People start spilling out. A skinny woman in bright colors who must be Philip's mother hands him one covered dish, and then gets out with another that she hands to my mother. Then she takes the covered dish from Mr. Mahavolich and he gets out the cooler. Mum takes Philip's mother into Grandma's kitchen.

Philip gets out with two huge teenagers who must be his brothers, though they look like they could be bodyguards. The blond one says, "Hi, bud, you Mitch? I'm Brad and this is Bruce. Your stepdad thinks you are the cat's aaa — pajamas, you know that?"

The red-haired one, Bruce, says, "Where should I put the steaks, Dad?" Mr. Mahavolich looks at Grandpa, and Grandpa points at Mr. Sloan's barbecue and says, "The carnivore grill is over there, but you can put that corn on the cob here if you want. There's butter and tin-foil in the kitchen." Then he introduces him-self and Mr. Sloan.

Mr. Mahavolich hands out drinks, and while Grandpa and Mr. Sloan make room for corn and steaks on their barbecues, they all talk about the game.

Grandpa is being awfully friendly, for him. He looks very neat with his pale-checked shirt. He ironed it this afternoon, and it looks sort of fresher than the other men's. He isn't frowning now. He kind of nods when he agrees with something the other men say. Mostly he's listening to the game, though. I notice he keeps the radio right beside him.

All this time Philip is standing by the van not saying anything. Bruce says, "Cat got your tongue, bud?" to him and sends him to the kitchen with a casserole. Just like that, and Philip doesn't sneer or anything.

I am really curious about Brad and Bruce. They don't seem at all like Philip. They are really friendly. I ask Bruce, the red-haired one, if he works at the garage. He says he works a few hours, but he's still in high school. He and Brad are in grade twelve, he says. So they must be twins, but I ask anyway and he says, "Yup." Bruce says he is going to be a mechanic and he hopes he'll be as good as Dan. Brad says the sooner he can wash the last of the grease off his hands the happier he'll be. Then there's this little pause and Brad asks, very casually, when the band is coming.

I say I don't know. Then, finally, my hot dog is ready and I take it to the kitchen to put ketchup on it.

Philip's there, hanging out with the women and not looking as sure of himself as usual. I could get to enjoy this.

6.

The three women are standing around, yakking. They hardly notice me come in. Mum is all dressed up in a flowery skirt and yellow tank top and her big earrings. She is tiny (my size is her fault!) but she looks like she is in good shape. She isn't, though. At least, she can't keep up with Grandma.

Grandma is fat and she is wearing this square pink blouse that makes her look even fatter than she is. Down there below her walking shorts her legs have blue veins and moles on them. She always wears running shoes, but she doesn't look athletic at all. She is, though. She runs almost every day and when Mum went with her once, Grandma left her in the dust. She even leaves me in the dust, but don't say I said so!

Mum finally sees me and introduces me to Philip's mother. Mrs. Mahavolich's face is a shock at first; it looks like she has dressed up like a clown. Just her face, not her clothes. It's her makeup. I am not used to makeup. It's true Mum experiments with her hair a lot. Once she actually shaved her head. But she never wears makeup and neither does Grandma.

Philip's mother is all bright colors. Her crinkly blouse is red and white stripes, her stretchy pants are red, and her face is all colors. Her cheeks are reddish, her lips are bright pink, her eyelids are blue and white. She has painted-on eyebrows and her eyelashes look sticky.

She smiles in a friendly way and says, "So you're Mitch. Dan says you have quite the imagination." What is Dan telling people about me?

I shake her hand and say, "Pleased to meet you, Mrs. Mahavolich," and she shrieks, "He's so polite! How did you make him so polite!" I back into a corner and make myself invisible. I shoot a glance at Philip. He is looking at his feet, and his ears are red.

No one mentions that Philip and I are in the same class. In fact, they ignore us. It seems the women are getting to know each other.

Mrs. Mahavolich says she does the books at the garage, so Grandma tells her she's a teacher and Tiffany (my mother) is a hairdresser.

Brad pokes his blond head in the kitchen and says, "Hi, Ms. Black" to Grandma and then asks his mother about plates and things. She throws him the van keys. Philip slinks out after his brother. I still haven't heard him say a word. I'm beginning to wonder if there are two sets of twins in the Mahavolich family, and Philip has been left at home while his quiet twin passes himself off as Philip. That would make sense. You'd think most people would leave Philip at home if they could.

As soon as Philip or the Philip-look-alike has gone, though, Mrs. Mahavolich sighs. "We worry about Philip," she says. "He doesn't have the gift of making friends like his brothers. He's so quiet, it's like he got dropped into the wrong nest."

Quiet! I almost choke on my last bite of hot dog, and I start coughing horribly. Mum frowns at me and points at the sink, so I pour a glass of water and try to drink some between coughs. Grandma says, "Brad and Bruce *are* very outgoing. They are a pleasure to teach too. I had them in my class last year. Does Brad still want to go to university?"

Mrs. Mahavolich brightens up a bit and says yes, and Bruce is still keen on the garage so Phil is happy. Then she sighs again, no doubt thinking sadly of Fill-up.

Mum asks me to help carry dessert out to the picnic table. It's been moved to the front lawn and the white plastic cloth is clipped to it. The plates are already there. I lugged them out there myself, this afternoon, as well as the cutlery, which weighs a ton, trust me. No paper plates or plastic forks because of the environment.

Mum's cheesecake is fantastic. I sit down with a big piece.

Philip is lurking by the van. Mum spots him. "Philip, would you like some cheesecake? Or a piece of pie?" she asks, being her usual friendly self at the wrong time. I've *told* her what Philip's like! Where's her loyalty? Whose side is she on, anyway?

I expect Fill-up to say, "Both!" but he looks disappointed and says, "I haven't had my dinner yet."

Mum says, "What should I save for you, then?" and he says, "Pie, please. Thanks, Mrs. MacLeod."

Mum smiles too. She says, "It's Ms.

MacLeod, Philip. There, that's your piece. I'll just set the serviette over it and here's a fork for you whenever you're ready."

I stare at Philip, but he just looks down and doesn't say anything. When my cheesecake is gone I make way for the carnivores. Philip and his brothers sit at the table with their steaks and corn. I'm too full for corn or baked potatoes, though they smell awfully good. Mr. Mahavolich gets more lawn chairs out of the van and everyone else starts to eat.

I decide to check out the rest of the street. Almost all the neighbors have done just like us, set out chairs and picnic tables and barbecues in the front yard. Except our house and one other, our whole street is old people whose kids are grown up and gone. Some even have grandchildren.

The other house with a kid is the Eccles'. They only have a baby. The baby is named Jennifer and she cries a lot. She likes me, though. Mrs. Eccles says I'm a miracle worker the way Jennifer stops crying when I show up. It doesn't work all the time. I mean, quite often I can't hear myself think around her. But apparently she cries less when I'm around than when I'm not. Scary thought! Mr. Eccles was in my mum's class at school. She says he's improved a lot since high school when he only had one thing on his mind and it wasn't calculus. He seems all right now. He calls me over and offers me a Coke.

I'm drinking the Coke and wandering back home when the Campbells and McAllisters drive up. Chevy's family has two names in it, just like Grandma and Grandpa's. She's McAllister like her mother, but her older sisters are Campbell like their father.

Chevy's full name is Siobhan Susan McAllister; the Susan is after my grandma, and Auntie Chris's middle name is Katherine after Ms. McAllister. But our family connection won't cut any ice with Chevy if she's still mad. She's like a force of nature. I wish I were like that. It's probably easier if you're tall. She's one of the tallest people in our class.

Mr. Campbell starts yelling hello to me while I'm still across the street. By the time I get there he's introducing himself and his family to the Mahavoliches at top volume, and then he's asking Mr. Sloan and Grandpa about the game. Meanwhile, he's unloading chairs and coolers, and Ms. McAllister and Grandma get out some covered dishes.

"Pull up some chairs, girls," says Grandma to Chevy's sisters. "You must know the Mahavolich boys from school, eh?"

Chevy's sisters are named Sinéad and Mairead, which both rhyme with "parade": "Shih-nade" and "Mah-rade." Ms. McAllister picked the kids' names in that family. She says there was always at least one other "Kathy" in school with her and she didn't want her kids to have such common names. You'd think she could have picked names people had heard of, though. Before she started calling herself Chevy, Siobhan used to get called things like See-oh-ban. It's supposed to be pronounced Sheh-VON.

Sinéad and Mairead sit down in lawn chairs and Brad and Bruce immediately get up from the picnic table and carry their desserts over to sit beside them. Sinéad is eighteen. She's quiet and sometimes she seems shy. She's the last person you'd expect to start a rock band. She's always friendly to me when it's just our families, but she's really quiet now. Mairead, who is seventeen, is doing all the talking. She has long dark brown hair and it has a new bright blue streak down one side. It makes her eyes look bluer, like someone splashed blue paint on them. Brad and Bruce are listening to her with like every pore. Brad actually drops his cheesecake off his fork and doesn't even notice the fork is empty when he puts it in his mouth.

I figure if these guys are going to pair up, Mairead should be with Brad, who has a long dangly earring and a ponytail. Sinéad looks more ordinary, so she should go with Bruce, who has a normal haircut and no visible tattoos or piercings.

Suddenly a voice says in my ear, "Truce for tonight, Midget, but look out tomorrow."

Of course it's Chevy. She's eating one of our veggie burgers. She's the only vegetarian in her family. I see *she* has a brand new streak in her hair too, but it's just blond, nothing too interesting.

I grab my chance. "It wasn't me who spilt the paint. It was Philip."

She chews and thinks. In case she doesn't believe me I say, "He said you were too dumb to figure it out." This is a lie and she suddenly squints at me.

"I don't think so. I don't think he said that. Did he?"

How could she tell? I shake my head. "No,

but he did spill the paint and blame it on me."

She chews and thinks some more. "Really?"

"Yeah."

"Huh," she says, and I wonder what that means.

7.

There's a roaring sound. An orange and white van rattles up the street — that is, a white van with lots of rust — with SPIKING A FEVER written on the side. It screeches to a stop behind Chevy's car. Sinéad and Mairead rush over, almost running into Grandpa, who starts grumping about the van being a "menace" with only its rust holding it together. Then he switches topics and gripes about Mairead's baggy clothes. "She'd be pretty if she'd dress like a girl." This is typical. He doesn't like Mairead's big shirt and pants, but when my mother wears dresses, Grandpa's always saying she looks cheap. He is always grumping about something. Everyone ignores him.

Spiking a Fever has two other members. Gaetan wears all black and lots of leather. He looks sinister, but he's always cracking jokes. He calls, "Hey, Chevy, how does a monster count to thirteen? On its fingers!" We groan. Then there's Lisa, who is the loudest girl I have ever met, including Chevy. She's like Mr. Campbell: why talk when you can yell? It's not like she's mad, either. She must be in heaven when she has a microphone. One side of her head is shaved today, the other is an orange ponytail. She has earrings all the way around the ear on the shaved side. Just looking at them makes me want to put ice on my own ear. I don't know how anyone can deliberately put holes in their own body. I'd probably faint and disgrace myself.

The band starts setting up, and Brad and Bruce offer to help. Dan says it's time to block off the ends of the street to cars. He gives me a stack of traffic cones, and he and Mr. Mahavolich take some sawhorses. It's pretty dark now. The traffic cones will reflect cars' headlights, and Dan wraps reflecting tape around the sawhorses too.

In the dark Philip is coming to life. He sneaks extra desserts from the Sloans. Then he runs by me and throws something into the Sloans' back yard.

Down the street there's some sort of commotion at the Eccles'. The baby is roaring. Mr. Eccles is walking her back and forth, fast, while Mrs. Eccles looks for something. Mrs. Eccles calls to me, "Mitch, help me look for Jennifer's soother. She won't sleep without it, and it's disappeared."

So I start hunting too. My appearance doesn't make Jennifer shut up this time. She doesn't even pause to draw breath. Mrs. Eccles picks up every single toy in the playpen and shakes out the blanket. I look under the lawn chairs and even start feeling in the grass with my hand.

"It was attached to her teddy bear so it wouldn't get lost in the dark." Mrs. Eccles sounds desperate. Mr. Eccles tries to hand her Jennifer, but Mrs. Eccles won't take her. I can't hear myself think over the crying. Mr. Eccles yells, "Take her, Jodi, I'll go to the store and buy another soother!" and Mrs. Eccles yells back, "No, I'll go."

Then Philip comes out of nowhere and holds up a blue teddy bear with a soother clipped to it.

"Is this what you're looking for?"

They treat him like he's a hero. Mrs. Eccles grabs the soother. She wipes it, jams it first in her own mouth and then in Jennifer's, all so fast you can't believe it. Jennifer shuts up, closes her eyes, and falls asleep. The silence is amazing. Mrs. Eccles takes Jennifer to put her to bed and Mr. Eccles sort of sags and then gets all jovial. He starts babbling, "What's your name, bud? You've just saved the day. Where did you find it, anyway?" He hands Philip a Coke and a whole bag of chips. Philip chomps and slurps. "My name is Philip Mahavolich, sir. The bear was just where Mitch threw it, in someone's back yard."

I am so shocked I'm speechless. Mr. Eccles stares at me and he seems speechless too. Philip says, "I'm sure Mitch didn't mean any harm, sir. It was probably just a joke."

I am ready to kill Philip. But before I can do anything the band starts warming up and we all just about jump out of our skins. Mr. Eccles says, "They'll wake the baby!" and tears off to talk to Mairead.

Philip smirks at me. I'm so mad I push him hard right in the gut. He falls over backwards, tipping over the edge of Jennifer's playpen. He lands on his bum right in the playpen! He starts yelling and so do I.

People stare at us. Philip's trying to get out of the playpen without spilling any more of his Coke and chips, and I keep pushing him back in. Then I feel heavy hands on my shoulders. It's Bruce. It doesn't hurt, but I can't get away either. He says, "Break it up, guys. Come listen to the band; they're pretty good." He waits until Philip is out and he's sure we're not going to fight anymore.

I am so upset I don't know what to do. So I go home. There's some cheesecake left. I sit on top of the picnic table and eat it and think how I have got to fix Philip. Spiking a Fever is playing a fast song and people are starting to dance. These are not people who live on our street — we have no teenagers on our street. But there they are, and now Mr. and Mrs. Eccles are dancing too. Chevy sits beside me. I feel so terrible I don't even think before I snarl, "What do *you* want?"

"What do you mean what do I want? What's the matter with you, Midget?"

I think about telling her to shove off. It would sound great — "Shove off, Siobhan." But instead I tell her what Philip did and how my neighbors, who I see practically every day of my life, will hate me.

Chevy is interested. "I thought it was too good to last, his being so quiet," she says. "Let's get back at him."

"Yeah, sure. Anything we could do to him, he'd do back to me only worse."

"Oh, come on. Don't be such a defeatist."

"Fine. How?"

"Well, what would he really hate?"

I'm stumped. What would Philip really hate? People liking him? Finding himself doing a good deed? Making his own lunch?

"That's it!!!!!" yells Chevy. "We'll booby-trap our lunches!"

"What do you mean?" I ask.

"Well, he's always stealing everyone's lunches. Let's put something awful for him to find. Say, a dead mouse."

"Or spiders and flies."

"Or we could spit on it and tell him after he's eaten it."

"I know!" I shout. "Something hot — hot pepper and spices. It wouldn't show but it would taste terrible!"

"Midget! You're brilliant!"

"We should get lots of people to do it so no matter whose lunch he steals it'll work."

"I'll tell Zoë and Nicky. Who else? We could

get the whole class in on it! We'll bring all his favorite things! We'll have to hide our real lunches . . ."

This is sounding pretty exciting. It could work. It really could. We go into the house and write down as many names from the class as we can. She says she'll phone the girls and I will phone the boys. We fold our lists and put them in our pockets.

"Shake on it," I say, and we do.

When we go back outside, lots of people are dancing to a slow song. Chevy's parents are holding onto each other and slowly lurching back and forth with each other. She groans. "Look at them."

The band changes to a fast number. Brad and a Goth girl show Grandma and Mr. Sloan how to shake their shoulders. Grandma laughs while she and Mr. Sloan copy them. The Goth's black full-length gloves make her almost invisible.

Then Dan and Mum run onto the street and I want to sink into the sidewalk. I know what's going to happen, and it does. They start jiving. They come close together, then back apart, Dan whirls Mum around and out, and then close to him. They are laughing. Gradually everyone else stops and watches. I think I am going to die of embarrassment. They are making a spectacle of themselves. And of me. In front of Chevy, sometimes my second-worst enemy, and recently, my ally.

"Just look at your mum and Dan! What are they *doing*?"

"It's called jiving," I mutter.

"Wow! Look at them go! How did they do that?"

Chevy actually likes it! She says, "They're great! Do you know how to do that? Show me!"

No way I'm dancing! I escape to the picnic table and watch Chevy dancing by herself until Bruce comes over and dances with her. Just about everyone I know is dancing. Grandma and Grandpa, even. Very close and slow. If I didn't know better I'd think they really liked each other, but this is Grandpa we're talking about!

After awhile I go upstairs to our kitchen and check out our supply of cayenne pepper.

In the morning when I get up there's no sign of Mum or Dan. I make toast and watch the Discovery Channel for awhile. Then I go downstairs.

Grandma and Grandpa are both up. I walk into their kitchen and Grandpa glares at me. Before he can say anything, Grandma says, "We're tired this morning, Mitch, can you come back later?" so I take the hint and make myself scarce.

I put on my favorite CD and get out my sketchbook. First I draw what happened with Philip and the soother. I never make Philip's body a stick-body because he's so big. I make it like a sausage. And his mouth I always draw really huge. He looks ridiculous in the playpen with his huge mouth open wide, throwing

Coke and chips into it. I draw a soother on a string around his neck and crack right up all by myself.

Then I draw what's going to happen when he steals our lunches tomorrow. I draw a bunch of kids: Richard with his cool baggy clothes (*his* sleeves are never too short!); Maria with her uncool baggy clothes; Daniel with his Game Boy; and Chevy with her henchwomen. I draw Chevy as a spring because she's always taking off in surprising directions. Zoë and Nicky I draw as Siamese twins because you never see one without the other. The real twins, Jake and Christopher Pfohl, I draw just ordinary, even though they're identical. Jake's hair is long, Christopher has a buzz-cut, so you can't tell they're identical, but apparently they are. At the cellular level.

I almost forget me, then I squeeze myself in by Daniel.

Then Philip. He's sitting on a hill of food. Chips, sandwiches, chocolate bars. I draw some open bags and make Philip's mouth wide open. Jagged lines show that his tongue is hot. I've heard spicy food makes your eyes water so I draw a few tears jumping out of his eyes. Then I draw a bottle of cold water that he can't get open fast enough. Boy, it all looks good. I hope it happens this way.

Mum and Dan finally get up at noon. Mum's eyes are half open. She sits at the table with a glass of juice and doesn't say a word. Dan and I make this huge brunch of hash browns and Spanish omelette and fruit cocktail. It's great. After we eat, Mum and Dan both pour coffee and sit back and look human. Mum reaches for Dan's hand and smiles at him. If they are going to be mushy, I'm out of here!

But Dan looks at me and asks in an ordinary voice, "How's school, Mitch?"

I wonder what to say. I could say, "It's the most fun I've had since I broke my arm and the bone poked through." I could say, "It's great if you like swimming with crocodiles and eating with future criminals." I could say, "School is the most cunning torture yet devised by the human mind."

Before I can decide, Mum says, "Your teacher phoned. She says you're getting extra help with your reading. Why didn't you say so? Should we practice at home?"

"No!" I say quickly. "I get enough help at school with Ms. Petrillo!"

Mum looks doubtful. "Maybe I should talk to her."

Dan asks, "How's everything else? Any new friends? No one giving you a hard time? Teacher okay?"

All these questions make me mad. "School is awful," I say flatly.

Dan looks concerned. He's about to go into his mother hen routine, I can tell, but Mum speaks first.

"Everyone has to do their time, Mitch. Look on the bright side, you've served six years already. With good behavior you might be paroled in only six more!" and she laughs. She tousles my hair while she does it.

Dan frowns at her. "Tiffany, it shouldn't be that bad. Maybe we should do something."

"Like what? Fast-forward him to age eighteen? School's the pits. He'll survive."

I feel depressed. I excuse myself from the table. I figure I might as well go and count tins in the blue box or something; it would be more fun than this conversation. Dan calls, "Let's read some more of *Lord of the Rings* this afternoon, Mitch." I say okay just to get rid of him.

I almost forgot: I have to make my phone

calls. Getting revenge on Philip is one thing about school that should be great. I only get through to three kids — the Pfohl twins, Jake and Christopher, and Tim Harbuckle. Some kids have too common last names to find in the phone book and two are out. Tim says he will phone some kids too, though, and when I call Jake he says he will too. Tim and Jake both love the idea, especially Jake. He often brings Cheezies, which are one of Philip's favorite things. For Philip, Cheezies are a whole food group. I say that and Jake snorts and laughs. He's mad, though. He hasn't even tasted a Cheezie in weeks. Then Christopher gets on the extension when I'm talking to Jake and he loves the idea too. It looks like Philip has made everyone mad.

I feel pretty good after the phone calls. I figure if Tim and Jake each get through to even one more kid that'll be six boys who will bring booby-trapped lunches. If six girls do too, that will be half the class.

Dan comes in when I'm thinking.

"Good to see you more cheerful, you had me worried," he says. He wants to read Tolkien. The hobbits are visiting the elves. Dan loves the elves. He reads with a lot of expression. I lie back in our La-Z-Boy and picture everything — the hobbits' hairy feet, the elves' shining.

Mum takes a break from her history book to listen too. She's reading *The Six Wives of Henry VIII*, but she says she could do with a little fantasy for a change, even if it is all about men. "An imagination like his but he can't write a book with two sexes in it," she grumps, as usual. But she likes Gandalf. So that's what we do most of the afternoon. It's peaceful.

Dan makes stir-fry for dinner, and we have ice cream cones for dessert. Then we take the Frisbee to the park. We look like a real family. We feel like one too. Who needs the Creep?

9.

In the morning I get this terrific idea. My mother isn't working this morning, so I ask if I can make a whole bunch of sandwiches and come home at noon to pick them up. She wants to know why, of course, but the great thing about Mum is she isn't nosy, so finally she just says, "Yes, okay," and I don't have to make up a lie about a school picnic or anything. Then she offers to drop them off if I like, which is even better. And when I ask if she could bring a bag of cookies too, she says, "Fine, can I polish your shoes while I'm at it?" but she isn't mad.

I pack all the hot things I can think of in my backpack: the black pepper and the cayenne pepper, and the hot mustard and the super-hot horseradish. I take off early for school.

Chevy, Nicky, Zoë and some other girls come early too. And Tim, Jake, Christopher and some other guys do too. Chevy has brought chili powder, which I didn't think of. We all get in this huge huddle and talk. Some of the kids haven't heard of the plan, so I show them the horseradish and stuff, and tell them Mum is bringing substitute sandwiches at noon. Daniel and a bunch of other kids get busy spicing up their lunches and snacks. They shake chili pepper onto their chips and spread mustard and horseradish in their sandwiches. Then I notice our huge group looks kind of suspicious so I say, "We better scatter!" and people kind of wander away in little giggling groups.

I can hardly wait until lunch. Somehow the morning crawls by. Ms. Petrillo notices something is up. "Is your birthday coming up, Mitch?" I shake my head. Even though I'm excited, the reading goes better. The words come clear in the right order, one by one, at least for awhile. It's such a peaceful room, Ms. Petrillo's. She says I'm making progress, and I can tell that's true. At home I'm reading an *Animorphs*, which is the first chapter book I've read by myself. Not much difference in Ms. Murphy's class, though.

During recess the last few kids in class hear about the plan. Richard threatens to tell Philip. I don't know how I get the nerve, but I say, "Fine, but don't be surprised if some day *your* lunch has chili pepper in it." He rubs his orange-dyed hair and looks at me. Then he says he won't tell. He looks at me differently too. No wonder. Richard is one of the cool kids. I never told him off before.

During math, which is right before lunch, Philip asks for permission to get something from his knapsack and we see his feet under the partition wandering from coat hook to coat hook. Some people giggle and the rest of us glare at them, but I feel like laughing myself when Philip swaggers back to his seat. I have to pinch a tiny piece of skin on my arm to keep from laughing.

The bell rings and I rush to wash my hands A.S.A.P. and meet Mum in the office. She has brought a package of licorice too. I love licorice. I carry everything upstairs and set it all on the floor outside our room. Inside, Philip's desk is covered with Vachon cakes, cookies, chips, Cheezies. Everything is in sandwich boxes or Ziploc bags. Nothing is in its own wrapper, but he doesn't seem to notice. He's biting into a sandwich, then he snarfs down some Cheezies. Everyone watches. No one says a word. Except for Philip's crackling and crunching, it is silent.

Suddenly his face goes all funny. His eyes get big and drops of sweat pop out of his skin. "AAAAowwww!" he howls. His lips look fiery red. He reaches for a can of pop and splashes it on his mouth. He looks like he might cry. I feel a little scared. What if he gets really hurt? Then Philip starts to get mad. He yells, "What's going on?" As soon as I see he's back to normal, I go get the food from the hall.

We all help ourselves and it feels like a party, except for Philip who is mad and snorting and whose mouth looks sore. The teacher on duty comes in. When she looks at his lips she tells him to go put ice on them. Then she stares around and asks what happened. No one says anything. It doesn't look like she's going to go away though. She waits.

I say, "Philip stole my lunch. I like lots of hot mustard, but maybe he's allergic to it."

Jake chips in, "I like spicy chips, and he stole those too."

Chevy says, "I brought curry and I can't find it."

10.

My full name is Mitchell Bryan MacLeod. Once after some kids were making fun of me at school for not having a father, I asked my mother if I was named after him. She looked at me like a worm had just crawled out of my nose. It turned out I am named after Bryan Adams, the singer. Mitchell isn't after anyone; it's my very own individual name.

"Why would I name you after that Creep? It is true I mistook him for a really nice guy, but boy, once you were on the way you couldn't see him for dust. He is like a shape shifter. Great guy one minute, slime ball the next. Only in his case the change is permanent. To this day his parents probably don't know about you. They were away a lot that summer. Well, never mind. Mitch, I liked you too much to name you after him."

I know this is true — the part about her liking me. I guess the rest must be true too. I have never seen my father, and according to my mother, he hasn't seen me. My mother doesn't like him (understatement of the year!) but she doesn't lie. Not even polite lies when you wish she would. That's why it drives her crazy when I lie. Which, as a matter of fact, I hardly ever do anymore. I made a New Year's resolution about it, but I don't think my mother has even noticed the improvement.

Auntie Chris and Uncle Brandon come for Sunday dinner. Megan couldn't come with Auntie Chris because she's delivering a baby. They make a big fuss over me, as usual. Auntie Chris gives me a surprise present for no reason! It's this big book about *Star Wars*. It has diagrams of the ships and lots of information about all the characters, and tons of pictures. It is a beauty. I sit down with it right away. I'm reading about the Death Star when Uncle Brandon comes into the living room and asks if I want to shoot some hoops. That's when I realize I've been reading for ages. Wow! And it was easy! As we walk out through the kitchen Auntie Chris says, "I'm glad I didn't wait for your birthday, Mitch." Me too! My birthday isn't until the end of May.

ıst want to. Where? Can I find him in
ne book or what?"

's over on Mary Street. It's his parents'
hey're in England for a year, and he's
the house while they're gone." Uncle
n takes another shot. "You didn't hear
me, though."

t's fine with me. Who would I tell? No
ks about the Creep, at least not to me.
eep whose real name is Ryan Carroll.
Uncle Brandon and Auntie Chris and
even Grandma and Grandpa all know.

one mentions Ryan Carroll again. Af-
per Dan comes over and we all play
oly. I clean up! I enjoy bankrupting
nd Auntie Chris and I'm not too sorry
Uncle Brandon, either.

cle Brandon grumps, "No one landed
yellows. Not once. You'd think by the
averages *someone* would have landed
m."

least you got hotels. I never got past
uses on my greens and two on the reds,"
ys.

ım gets up to make coffee. "Should I
um up for coffee?" she asks. "Chris?
ɔn?"

Uncle Brandon and I are in the driveway
when I remember the basketball is in my room.
Grandpa yelled at me for leaving it lying around
down here. So I run up the outside stairs, but
I don't go in because I hear my name. I can
see Mum's back through the curtains. She's
standing at the counter across from the sink.
The water is running hard into the spaghetti
pot. Auntie Chris must be over by the stove.
Her hand reaches over and turns off the tap.

"Mitch should know, Tiff," Auntie Chris is
saying.

What should I know?

"If he wants to know his son, he knows
where we are," snaps my mother, in a hard
voice that she only ever uses when she talks
about the Creep.

"I think he'd like to know him, but he's
ashamed of himself."

"So he should be."

"Think of Mitch. He must have questions."

"He has Dan. Dan loves Mitch like he is
his own, and they get along like a house on
fire. As you know. Anyway, what's all this about
Ryan Carroll all of a sudden?"

Ryan Carroll. My father's name is Ryan
Carroll.

Auntie Chris says, "He's joined our firm. I see him every day."

My mother's back freezes. "I can't believe this. When?" Then, without waiting for an answer, she swings around and glares at Auntie Chris. "I sure hope you aren't talking about me!"

"Of course not! Cool your jets! Geez, Tiffany, aren't you tired of being poor? Mitch is his kid too, and he makes good money now. Get him to pay support, for Pete's sake. You could go back to school if you want. Take that chef's course you were interested in."

"I'm not taking that Creep's money. No amount of money can pay for the last eleven years."

That sounds bad. Do they have to be paid for? That's my whole life. I feel sick.

"I know that. I know. But it would be a start. I could arrange it all if you like, I do this stuff every day for a living . . ."

"No! And don't you dare mention it to Mitch!"

I feel like I've been standing there for about a hundred years. I don't know what to do. I'm all hot and churned up inside, but at the same time I'm frozen to the spot. I can't move. Then

Uncle Brandon yells, "H
kitchen window is open,
and sees me there. Fina
ing, running through th
ball, and back out agai
thing. Mum calls me, but
down the outside steps
voices, "Now look . . ."
to listen this time.

Uncle Brandon and
and finally I calm dowr
around the driveway and
but net!

"Way to go!" says Unc
a shot too. Then he tos
comes after it, but I kee
long enough to take and
circles the hoop lazily onc
and then falls through.

"Uncle Brandon, d
Carroll?" I ask.

He takes another sho
rage!" he jokes. Fools aro
bit.

Finally he says, "Sure."
"Where does he live?"
"Why do you want to

"I j
the ph
"H
place.
living i
Brandc
it from
Th
one ta
The C
Who
maybe
No
ter su
Mono
Mum
about
Ur
on my
law o
on the
"A
two h
Dan s
M
ask N
Brand

Everyone says sure so I phone down and talk to Grandma. She says she'll be right up. I wonder if Grandpa will come, but it turns out he's watching the never-ending game.

Unfortunately, people start talking about me and school.

"How'd the meeting at the school go?" Grandma asks Mum. "Was Kathy there, or any other parents?"

It's more than two weeks since Philip stole the spicy lunches. Ms. Murphy and the principal found out what happened and they wanted all the parents to come in to a meeting, but Mum couldn't get to a meeting until Friday. I haven't asked her about it, and she hasn't said anything.

Now she tells everyone all about it, and I fidget. I haven't figured out yet whether she's mad at me. It wouldn't be bad if she was mad now, because she feels bad about what I heard about the Creep, so she wouldn't get *too* mad. Also, to be honest, I'm kind of mad at her.

"Kathy was there, and Shirley Mahavolich, and some other parents. It seems Philip has been stealing kids' lunches and snacks all year. Right, Mitch?" I nod. Mum goes on, "Anyway, the other kids got fed up and spiked their lunches with horseradish and chili and such and just waited for Philip to steal them. I guess that taught him a lesson, all right."

Auntie Chris laughs. "Good for you, Mitch."

Grandma shakes her head. "It is so hard to catch a child who steals. What did the teacher have to say?"

"Oh, she tried to sit on the fence. On the one hand, Philip obviously shouldn't be stealing, but on the other hand it was mean of the kids to set him up."

"Did you let her get away with that, Tiff?" asked Dan with a smile.

"No way! I said to Shirley, 'No offence but your boy's been giving mine grief all year and this stealing is the last straw.' I said I was proud of all the kids for solving a problem the teacher couldn't handle by herself. Of course, Ms. Murphy didn't like that, but it was true." Mum smiles at me. "Way to go, kid."

Dan is looking a little worried. "What about Shirley and Phil? It would be a shame if there was bad feeling over the kids."

Mum shrugs. "Shirley says she doesn't understand it. She wanted me to promise that it wouldn't happen again. I said, it sure won't happen as long as Philip keeps his hands off other kids' things."

Dan groaned. "Oh, Tiff, couldn't you have been a little more tactful?"

"No."

Grandma says, "I think it will be okay, Dan. Shirley and Phil must know Philip is in trouble at school. This isn't the first time and it won't be the last."

Uncle Brandon gets up to go. He says he'll look in on Grandpa to say goodnight. Ruffles my hair and says, "Keep in touch, eh, bud? I'm just a phone call away."

Dan and Mum start cleaning up dishes, and Auntie Chris and Grandma are talking in low voices in the living room, so I decide to go to bed. I need a few things, first, though. I look up an address in the phone book. Then I get the city map and take it to my room with my *Star Wars* book.

11.

There's no chance to do anything with Ryan Carroll's address and phone number right away. School gets really busy. Even though I take work to Ms. Petrillo's room to work on with her, I still have lots of homework. Ms. Murphy assigns a big project on prime ministers and sends a math drill home every single day.

So it's November before I go look at the Creep's house. I go on a Saturday afternoon while Mum is at work. I promised her I'd go outside and I do. The Creep's house is on Mary Street near Union. It's about ten minutes' walk from the school, which is ten minutes from my house. It turns out to be an ordinary brick house with a fence around the back yard and a flash red car in the driveway. I sit on a bench at the bus stop across the street and look at the house. Then I go home.

I do this a couple more Saturdays, only I hide behind a tree. The third time, a man comes out of the house. He's a surprise. He is *big*. As tall as Dan, but not so dumpy. I could draw him as a triangle on legs with the wide part for his shoulders. He walks like an athlete, light on his feet, graceful. He gets in his car and drives right past me. He has short hair and a gold earring.

I feel pretty strange. I have probably just seen my father. He doesn't *look* like the kind of person who wouldn't want to know his own son. He looks nice. His hair is light-colored like mine. And he is definitely big.

When Mum's hair isn't pink it is brown. Not really dark, but darker than mine. And her eyes are brown too. And as I have mentioned, she isn't big and neither am I. How could a very big person have a very small child? Is that possible? Or is it only temporary? Maybe there's hope for me yet.

All weekend I think about Ryan Carroll, my father. My stomach gets butterflies in it that won't go away. They are happy butterflies, though. I am thinking about going to meet him by myself. Why not?

But then I get thinking about that flash car. Cars cost a lot of money. Even second-hand cars like Dan's. A brand new car like that would cost more than Mum makes in a whole year, probably. And though she never blames me, I know she could have got a better-paying job if she didn't have me to take care of.

Why should the Creep have a flash car and a job with lots of money when my mum doesn't have any car and has a job that doesn't pay very much and that she doesn't even like?

That is a completely new thought. I never thought that before, about Mum's job, but suddenly I realize it's true. She doesn't like being a hairdresser. And now I don't want to meet the Creep. Even if we have the same color hair, he doesn't even know that, does he? He hasn't even bothered to find out.

And Mum is great, really. If I go looking for the Creep she might think she's not enough for me. She might think I'm unhappy with her.

I read my *Star Wars* book and then my stars book, but I can't stop thinking about that car and that house. A whole house for one person.

12.

Ever since he stole the pepper lunches and burnt his mouth, Philip has been worse. He makes Maria cry one day just by yakking on about her clothes. He has a go at lots of kids, but not all of them. Not Richard or Chevy, for instance. Just about everyone else, though. Unfortunately, he has favorite targets, and I am one.

I dread school, I really do. My stomach feels bad almost all the time, except weekends. I start getting headaches too, and Mum wonders if I need stronger glasses. I just got new ones before school started and she's worried how she's going to afford another pair. But when I go for an eye exam after school, my eyes are fine. That's the good news.

The bad news is practically everything else.

Like reading buddies. It isn't until the end of November that our class starts meeting their reading buddies while I am with Ms. Petrillo, so I am spared the ordeal of having six-year-old Brittany read to *me*. Believe me, you do not know what humiliation is until you have had a grade one reading buddy who reads better than you do.

Philip is pursuing me relentlessly. The worst thing about Philip, if I had to pick just one thing, is that he gets everyone else laughing at me too. And everyone, except the teacher, calls me Midget.

Whenever the teacher calls on me Philip makes this "Wah! Wah!" sound that's supposed to be a baby crying, so it is hard to think. Ms. Murphy makes him miss recess all the time, but he doesn't care. At least recess is a Philip-free zone!

And so is Ms. Petrillo's room. Something wonderful happens there. It's so different. She doesn't even talk. And the room is empty, so it's really quiet. And the words come clear. One day I read a long thing about the ancient Mayans out loud and I get every word right, except I pronounce some wrong, like "Mayan," which is a trick word. It isn't pronounced like it's spelled. It's "my" not "may." Ms. Petrillo asks me questions about the Mayans afterwards and gets me to write some things down. And I do it all. Just like at home when I'm reading my *Star Wars* book. I discover this: when reading works, it's a very calm feeling, like a stream running all in one direction without bumps.

After the Mayan thing, I do my class reading homework, and then we go over my prime minister book. It takes a whole week. I can't believe how great I'm doing. I want to tell everyone. But no one at school would believe me because in Ms. Murphy's class I am still the kid who can't read. Sometimes when it's seat work it goes fine, but no one but Ms. Murphy knows that.

At least Chevy leaves me alone now. She's too busy liking Richard. At recess she stands under the tree and giggles about him to the henchwomen, and over by the swing Richard's friends bug him about her. Chevy and Richard never seem to talk to each other, though.

One day Richard calls me over.

"You're friends with Chevy, eh?"

"No," I say.

"Doesn't her family know your family or something?"

"Yeah, but that doesn't mean anything."

Richard ignores this. "The thing is, I need someone to give her a message."

I stare at him. Richard is one of the cool kids. He can do anything. He's excellent at every sport and he's not actually *bad* at anything.

"Come on, Midget," he says, when I don't say anything. "You do me this favor and I'll do you a favor."

"Like what?"

"What do you want?"

I have to think about this. Having the coolest boy in the class offer to do me a favor — *beg* to do me a favor! — sn't something that's going to happen every day. Finally I decide. I say, "You know how Philip's always giving people a hard time?"

He nods.

"And he tries to make everyone else laugh?"

"Yeah, what about it?"

"Well, don't laugh, and don't let your friends laugh, either."

"Okay, that's easy. I promise. Now here, give her this, okay? In private, away from Zoë and Nicky. And don't you read it, either, I'll be watching!"

He sticks this hard ball of paper in my hand.

It's been folded so often it's a tiny cube. I don't care what's on it. I'm not interested in his pathetic lovesick ramblings.

I walk straight up to Chevy. As usual she is in the middle of a bunch of girls. They all stop talking and look at me.

"I've got something for you from Richard," I say.

She sticks out her hand. "So give, Midget."

I shake my head.

"Over there. He said I have to give it to you alone."

All the girls giggle like a bunch of idiots. No one said anything funny, did they? Chevy gets kind of pink. She straightens up and strides away from everyone, so I follow.

"Give!" she says.

I shake my head. She starts getting mad, so I hurry what I have to say. "I give you this, you have to do me a favor."

"Okay, okay." She tries to grab my hand, so I put it behind my back.

"What do you *want*?" Chevy's teeth are grinding together, and her eyes are getting mean. I get her to promise the same thing Richard did, then I toss her the ball of paper and take off.

It helps some. The next time I freeze in front of the map and can't read "Toronto," Philip does his usual "Wah! Wah!" but the laughter isn't as loud as usual. Richard even mutters, "Grow up, Mahavolich."

I still look forward to weekends, though, and soon there's something better to look forward to: we're coming up to Christmas break — almost three weeks of no school.

13.

Christmas at our house is really nice, even if I am the only kid. Uncle Brandon and Auntie Chris and Megan always come for part of the day. Dan too, of course. Everyone makes something special to eat. Even Grandpa isn't usually too bad at Christmas. By now everyone at home has noticed that I am doing a lot of reading in my spare time, so I'm pretty sure some of my presents are going to be books. I've hinted I'd like the other *Star Wars* book and my fingers are crossed.

We get off school a week before Christmas. Grandma is still teaching. In fact, she's staying late to mark papers, so I am alone at the house a lot. Uncle Brandon comes over Monday afternoon to keep me company. We play chess and listen to my favorite CD. Uncle

Brandon likes my favorite singer, too. He thinks she's very talented. He's right. She's an incredible dancer as well as singer. So at least one member of my family has good taste!

Tuesday Uncle Brandon picks me up so we can finish our Christmas shopping. I have already got Dan a winter baseball hat with earflaps so he won't freeze at work. At the mall I buy Grandma a headband for her jogging, and for Grandpa I get a cover for the TV guide. Kind of lame, but it's all I can think of.

I want to get Mum something really good. There's this book she might like. Uncle Brandon has heard of it and he thinks it's a great idea. Unfortunately, even in paperback it's more than $1.50, which is what I'm down to: $1.63 to be exact. I tell Uncle Brandon my problem.

"Do you think I could borrow the money from you? I could pay you back some every Saturday."

But even though it's Christmas, he says no. No way he's lending his favorite nephew money. "'Neither a borrower nor a lender be,'" he says.

This is terrible! Why didn't I plan better? Mum's present should be the best, and now it looks like all I'll be able to get her is a lousy bookmark or something.

Then Uncle Brandon hands me a twenty-dollar bill. "Keep it," he says. Twenty dollars! I can't believe it. I get this measly allowance; it's not too often I've seen twenty dollars at once. Never except my birthday, in fact. My mouth is still hanging open; I haven't even thanked him.

"Thank you!" I say and I can feel this huge grin coming. He smiles back and gives me a sideways hug.

Now I can buy Mum's book and still have almost twelve dollars left over. So if by any chance no one gives me that other *Star Wars* book it shouldn't be too long before I can buy it myself. Once I've got her book and Uncle Brandon has bought a CD for Auntie Chris, we look around the mall a bit. I tell him about this game I'd like for my Game Boy. It's new and it's already sold out (but there's always my birthday!) Then we eat chips from New York Fries and drink Coke. I love chips.

It's a nice week, coming up to Christmas. Wednesday, Uncle Brandon comes for the morning. Before he goes home at lunchtime, he asks what I am going to do in the afternoon.

When she left for work, Mum gave me strict instructions to play outside for awhile. She says that every day. She's keen on fresh air. For me, but not for herself.

I said, "*You* don't go outside every day! Don't you think that's a bit hypocritical?"

She called me a smart alec. Some people. You just can't reason with them. I'll get some fresh air, all right.

I tell Uncle Brandon I will watch TV some and maybe read. But really I'm going to spy on Ryan Carroll's house as soon as it's dark.

Up to now I've only been there three times, always on Saturday. Now it gets dark so early I just go and sit on that park bench in plain sight, noticing different things. All the windows are dark and the driveway is empty, but there are Christmas lights along the eaves and I wonder what colors they are. Grandma is home when I get back and she asks where I've been. I say I visited Dan at the garage.

I go again on Thursday. This time the car is in the driveway and there are lights on in the house. Also, the Christmas lights are on. Red and white. All along the roof and the big window. I can see through the open living room curtains that in the back of the house is the kitchen, and he is moving around in there. He's cooking.

I don't know what makes me decide to ring the doorbell, but all of a sudden that is what I am doing. I run up to the front door and stand there like an idiot for a minute, terrified. Then I ring the bell and take a huge deep breath. I can hear music being turned down inside, and footsteps coming. Then he is standing in the doorway, looking down at me.

The first thing I notice is his earring. Also, he's wearing an apron, which might have been funny another time, but right now my mouth is dry as cardboard and my heart is racing. The next thing I notice is his face looks shocked.

We both stand there for a couple of years and then he shivers and asks me if I want to come in. So I go in, and he shuts the door behind me and I stand there some more while we stare at each other. There's a nice smell of tomato sauce or something. The Crash Test Dummies are singing from the kitchen.

Finally he says, "Mitch, right? I'm Ryan. Pleased to meet you." He sticks out his hand for me to shake and then notices it has flour on it and takes it back and wipes it on his apron. I take off my mitten and we shake hands.

"Do you want to come back to the kitchen with me? I'm in the middle of something. Or if you like I can go turn the stove off and we can sit in here. I assume you want to talk to me, is that right?"

I don't know if I want to talk to him or not. Here I am in this stranger's house and no one knows where I am. I have no idea what to say to him.

"I've got to go," I say, and I open that door and run.

14.

Friday is Christmas Eve. Everyone goes to Auntie Chris and Megan's apartment. Megan's last name is Ito. When I first heard her name I was just a kid and I thought it was all one word. I said, "Pleased to meet you, Meganito," and everyone laughed except Megan. I liked her right away.

Uncle Brandon brings someone we haven't met before. Her name is Lindsay and she talks to me like I am seven years old.

"What do you want from Santa Claus?" she asks in a sickly sweet voice, bending over to be at my level. I glare at her. She doesn't get it, so I just ignore her.

"Oh!" she says, "He's shy. Isn't that cute?"

Aargh!

We always have take-out food on Christmas Eve, with homemade desserts. Auntie Chris has made shortbread cookies and there's half-hour pudding in the oven. It smells great. It has brown sugar sauce, which is so sweet it makes Mum's teeth ache, but not mine! Uncle Brandon and Lindsay bring the take-out. It's Italian this year. It smells so good!

Auntie Chris brings out a bottle of wine and there is just enough for her to pour some into every glass, including a little bit in mine.

She lifts her glass. "Peace on earth, kindness in families."

Auntie Chris practices family law and Christmas is one of her busiest times because of families fighting. Mum and Dan seem especially happy, as though they have a secret. Once Mum even giggles, which is a little suspicious.

We play cards. Megan is awfully good at cards. First we play Thirty-One, and she knocks with only fourteen points and wins! Grandpa perks up. He loves a challenge. He and Megan eye each other, trying to figure out who's bluffing. Auntie Chris's beeper goes once, but she doesn't have to go out. She says, "I'm on call tomorrow, but Ry — one of my colleagues is on call tonight."

Megan is off for a week over Christmas.

She is a doctor. She says for once she can stay up as late as she likes.

Uncle Brandon says he might have to move this summer. He's got a job interview in January up in North Bay. It sounds like he wants the job, but things sure would be different without him. His car needs a tune-up before he goes for the interview, so he and Dan figure out when he should take it in.

So far the music has all been Sarah MacLachlan. She is not my personal favorite; that's all I'll say. Grandma wants a change. (Thank you! Thank you! Thank you!) "Let's have some Christmas carols, eh?" She gets up to change the CD, but three other people beat her to the CD player. Mum and Dan and Uncle Brandon each want something different. Finally they put on Enya singing Christmas carols.

Uncle Brandon leaves to drive Lindsay home.

"Will Uncle Brandon come back?" I ask.

"You bet. It's early yet. We haven't even gone for our walk," Grandpa says. Grandpa really likes Christmas. He used to dress up as Santa Claus for Mum, Uncle Brandon, and Auntie Chris when they were little, though personally I find that hard to believe.

We decide to play Pictionary while we wait for Uncle Brandon. Grandpa sits out so it's even numbers. Megan and I clean up. We only miss one. She loves my drawing. It is true that she is lucky to have me. When we have to draw "wet" Grandma draws raindrops and Auntie Chris draws a bunch of things that you can't tell what they are. They're supposed to be a wet floor and wet clothes. I draw a dripping sponge and Megan gets it with a little time to spare.

Auntie Chris thinks Megan is pretty good at drawing too, but she really isn't. You should see her drawing for "jump." It looks like someone with a stomachache! And for "mortgage" she draws a house with someone standing beside it who is supposed to be crying. I don't even know what a mortgage is, so that one wasn't really fair. It's the only one we miss. We win anyway.

Uncle Brandon still isn't back. While we're waiting we may as well have some fun, so I say, "Maybe we should open our presents."

I suggest this every year, and every year everyone says, "Wait until tomorrow." Sure enough, there's a chorus of "Wait until tomorrow!"

Uncle Brandon comes in with snow in his hair.

"Let's go for our walk now. It's snowing great big flakes. And if we wait too long the roads will be bad when we go home."

It is peaceful in the snowy night. The snow-flakes are huge. The sky is black like ink. Auntie Chris and Uncle Brandon walk ahead. Megan and Dan lag behind. They're talking about how to build up the NDP. Dan says it needs a tune-up. Megan says it needs more than a tune-up; it needs CPR. Grandma and Grandpa are just ahead, talking in low voices. Once they chuckle, and Grandma takes Grandpa's arm.

Even though everyone's talking, the falling snow muffles their voices. It is magical. Mum grabs my hand and swings it and I let her. She is marching along in her big pink coat. Her toque covers her hair and snow lands on it. She tilts her head back and sticks out her tongue to catch some snowflakes. "Mitch, I got one! You try it!"

She is a very unusual mother, I think.

15.

Christmas morning I am awake at six. There is no point getting up this early. Mum and Dan's brains are on-timers. They can't be booted up before eight on a holiday, and then it takes coffee already made to do it. I lie in the dark for awhile, feeling Christmas morning lying all around, waiting for us.

Even though I can't see the Christmas tree from my bed, I can picture the lights glowing in the dark. On Christmas Eve we always leave the lights on all night, so that's the first thing we see when we get up. The whole house feels full of happiness just waiting to be born. Anything could happen. Finally I get up and tiptoe to the living room to look at the tree. It looks so beautiful and peaceful. The soft colors shine in the dark and none of the scuff marks on the furniture show up. The pile of presents looks mysterious, even though I've shaken every one.

At one minute to eight o'clock I pour two cups of coffee and put them on the tray and carry them to Mum's room. I balance the tray on one hand and knock on the door with the other.

"Mmmmffff?" calls someone; I can't tell who.

"Merry Christmas!" I call brightly, opening the door and walking in with the coffee.

"What time is it?" Mum mumbles.

Dan sits up. He wakes up faster than Mum. "Merry Christmas, Mitch! Thank you very much, this will hit the spot. Tiffany, it's eight o'clock and Mitch has brought us coffee."

Mum sits up, but she doesn't want her coffee yet. She gets her housecoat on and takes the coffee to the living room. We all sit looking at the tree. It's starting to get light out now so I open the curtains. I don't say too much until they've had their first cup — my mother is really grumpy first thing in the morning, Christmas or no Christmas. But when Dan brings their second cups in, Christmas really starts. I sort through the presents and hand them out.

There are quite a few for me.

The first one I open is from Uncle Brandon. It is fairly small and flat and square . . . Yes! It's a Game Boy game! In fact, it's the new one I thought I couldn't get until my birthday! Wow! All the time I was telling him about how it was sold out he must have already got it. After the twenty dollars, I didn't expect to get anything from him.

Then from Dan I get my very own set of Tolkien: *The Hobbit* and *The Lord of the Rings* all in a box. It's quite a while since we read *The Hobbit*; maybe I'll start that. They'll never believe their eyes if they see me reading it by myself!

Mum's is big but thin and flat. It's the other *Star Wars* book! Then there's a box from her too, and it's a new pair of running shoes. I've been needing some because there is a hole in my gym shoes. Then there is a very big present from Grandma and Grandpa, which will be clothes. Yup, it's a new parka. So my wrists won't stick out of the sleeves any more and freeze. This one is a three-way parka: the lining unzips and then you have two jackets instead of one. Also, the sleeves zip off the nylon part so you can wear it as a vest over the lining. It's black, and the lining is red with black trim. I will definitely have to thank Grandma for this.

The last present is from Auntie Chris and Megan. It turns out to be two presents in one. It is a big, soft parcel, which turns out to be two pairs of jeans. In the pocket of one of the pairs of jeans is another little present, a Swiss Army knife. There is a note with it. "If you take this to school we will deny all knowledge of it!!! Enjoy it everywhere else. Love, Auntie Chris and Megan."

This knife is incredible. It has a gazillion blades. There are three knife blades, a corkscrew, a pair of scissors, and some things that I don't know what they are for. It even has a toothpick and a tiny pen! I can't believe it's mine.

I thank Mum and Dan and look at all my presents again. I am even glad about the clothes. I only have three pairs of pants not counting these new jeans. One pair I've really outgrown. My blue track pants are so short I don't wear them to school. Whenever Chevy saw them last year she called them "floods" because supposedly I could wear them in a flood and they wouldn't even get wet. Ha ha.

So the jeans are good. And with the money Uncle Brandon gave me, maybe I can buy a sweatshirt, since Mum gave me the *Star Wars* book.

Dan and Mum like my presents too. Dan says the hat is a brilliant idea. He says a toque's no good for keeping the sun out of his eyes, and a baseball hat lets his ears freeze, but the hat I got will be perfect. Mum is very interested in her book. She wonders where I heard of it. I tell her Megan was telling Auntie Chris about it ages ago.

"Isn't Moab a place?" she asks, looking at the title. "How can a place be a washpot?" I can tell she is dying to start reading it, but instead we get dressed and have breakfast.

After that, we all read. Mum has given Dan a book too, so we all have something new. It doesn't occur to me until later that Dan didn't give Mum a present. Everyone is coming over around three. At two thirty Dan sits beside me on the couch. I'm busy with my Game Boy so he has to wait a minute to talk to me. Then he says, "Mitch, can we talk for a minute?" and Mum walks in too.

Uh-oh. Something's up. Something bad? It doesn't seem to be. I'm trying to read their faces and they definitely aren't mad. A little worried, maybe.

Mum says, "Mitch, Dan and I have a surprise for everyone, but we thought you should know ahead of time."

I wait.

Mum looks uncomfortable. "The thing is, you know Dan and I have been seeing each other for a long time."

She stops and I wait some more, but I am beginning to see the light. Their secretive giggles at Auntie Chris's come back to me.

Dan says, "For Christmas I am giving your mother a ring, Mitch. It's an engagement ring. We're going to get married."

He looks so solemn and still a little worried, that for a minute I want to laugh. Then I want to play a joke. Like, I could say, You mean you're asking my permission? Well, what if I say no? Will you forget about it?

But I don't. I say, "What took you guys so long?"

Well, you should see their faces. They are a series of pictures: Surprise. Relief. Happiness. They get these big dumb smiles on their faces, and I probably have a big dumb smile on my face too.

"Oh, Mitch! Are you really glad?" Mum is a little teary. She throws her arms around me in one of her fierce hugs, and Dan hugs us both, and that's how Grandma and Grandpa find us.

So then they tell Grandma and Grandpa, and Dan gives Mum her ring, which it is obvious to me she has seen before, but she gets all emotional anyway. Everyone else comes then and there's all this excited talk. Dan gets a bottle of champagne out of the fridge so we can all drink toasts to their (and our!) happiness.

At one time or another during the afternoon I catch everyone except Megan eyeing me in a thinking way and I know they are wondering How I Am Taking The News. They're nuts. What's not to be glad about? Dan's here half the time anyway.

Grandpa corners me while dinner is being dished up.

"Mitch, I hope you realize this is a Very Good Thing."

Just in case he's considering giving one of his rare but oh-so-long-and-dull lectures I agree with him, which is the fastest way to head him off. "Yes, Grandpa." It doesn't work.

"And I hope you will welcome Dan to your

family. He is good for your mother, and, I might add, good for you too, and it's about time they decided to do the Right Thing. Now they have, let's all make it as easy as possible."

"Yes, Grandpa," I say again, but I am getting restless. Also grumpy.

"No acting up, young man. No causing trouble. It isn't an easy situation, so we all have to do our part to make it work. You understand?"

What does he mean? I never cause trouble. What's not an easy situation? If you ask me, the only difficult part of the situation is Grandpa. I'm sick of him treating me like a moron.

Grandpa stares at me.

I glare back.

Sometimes I hate Grandpa. I really do. If there is a God I must be a major sinner. Grandpa sure thinks so, and he talks quite a bit about God. But if God is like the way he describes, I don't think I would like God much either, if I met Him. Or Her. Even if today is Jesus' birthday I'm mad at Him too. Not the baby Jesus, of course, but the grown-up one who died for people like Grandpa.

Sometimes Mum and I talk about it. She says Grandpa is living proof that people see

God "through a glass, darkly." She figures Grandpa's window is so dark it must have been boarded up. I hope she's right. But then Mum has her own ideas that no one else seems to have. She doesn't have any use for church. And she calls God "She," and says she hopes when she's dead she can buy God a beer and ask Her a few hard questions. Then she figures she and God will have a good laugh together and be friends. When she says things like that it makes Grandpa boil. I know there's only supposed to be One True God, but in my house it seems like there must be at least two.

The food is on the table. Luckily, I can't even see Grandpa from my end of the table. The card table is set up next to the kitchen table, and a big cloth makes them look like one long table that goes from the kitchen through the archway into the living room. There are eight of us, and I can see everyone else but Grandpa so after awhile I don't feel so upset. I'm sitting across from Auntie Chris. Megan is on one side of me and Dan is on the other. Now and then Dan turns to me and grins. Once he puts his arm around me and says, "You've given me the best Christmas present, bud. We couldn't be this happy if you weren't so happy for us."

By now I've had some time to think. "So Dan, you aren't going to change, are you?"

"What do you mean?" He's taken his arm away and we're both back to eating, but he's listening all right.

"Well, I know you'll live here and everything, but you aren't going to start bossing me around are you?"

Good old Dan. He doesn't miss a beat. "Worried I'll turn into the evil stepfather, eh? No way. You seem to do a great job of bossing yourself most of the time. The rest of the time it's up to your Mum."

So that's all right, then, and not counting Grandpa it's been a pretty good Christmas over all.

16.

Mum and Dan are both off work until Wednesday. So we have three days at home, all three of us. Dan goes back to his apartment for clean clothes, but otherwise he stays here. It's like practice for when they are married, I guess.

He and Mum sleep in late and take ages to get going once they are finally up, but then we all do something. On Sunday we play cards and go for a walk. On Monday it snows, so we take Dan's toboggan and my sled to the school hill. We have races to the bottom. It is great having parents — well, *a* parent and Dan — who like to do stuff. Chevy's parents are so old they are more like grandparents. They don't do anything.

All the same, our apartment feels awfully full. There's always someone in the bathroom.

And every time I go from one room to another I meet someone. Also, it's amazing Dan isn't worried Mum will have second thoughts. Like when he cuts his horrible thick toenails in the living room — ugh! Who wants to watch that? I'm not used to having him here so much. What it will be like after the wedding?

On Tuesday, Dan goes home after supper — finally! — and he isn't coming back tonight. Mum is scrubbing the kitchen floor. I figure we'd better talk.

"Mum, maybe we should get a bigger apartment if Dan's going to live with us."

"Kind of crowded with the three of us, eh?" she says, but she doesn't answer me.

"Well?" I prod after ages. She must have forgotten what we're talking about. The floor is finished. She backs out of the kitchen with the pail, takes off her rubber gloves.

"Dan wants to buy a house. He has the down payment saved. But I don't know. It would be expensive."

"A house! You never said we might be moving!"

"Well, we're thinking of buying a house, but we haven't decided. We haven't even looked at any."

"You should have told me we might move."

"Yeah, well. Would you like a house of our own?"

"Probably, but it depends where it is."

"We won't do anything without talking to you first, Mitch."

She'll do it too. She doesn't just say what you want to hear like Joey's mother used to do. I don't know how I feel about maybe moving, though. I'd miss Grandma if we moved very far. Not Grandpa, though. We *could* use more room, and maybe we'd move out near Daniel. Or Joey. That might be good. That's what I'll say if they start looking at houses.

So I stop worrying and go read some *Hobbit*. I can't believe how easy it is to read at home now. I'm reading like three books right now, what with *The Hobbit* and the new *Star Wars* and this *Sherlock Holmes* collection I found on the shelf. If only I could read at school too!

Next day Mum goes to work and I have the apartment to myself. Right after breakfast I go over to Ryan Carroll's and ring his bell. He doesn't come to the door, but I can hear music so I stand there and ring it every few minutes until suddenly the door jerks open.

There he is in a bathrobe. Wet hair, gold necklace, bare feet. Looks mad until he sees who it is. Then his face changes.

"You better come in. It's freezing."

Once I'm in and the door's closed he says, "Take your coat off and have a seat, eh? I've got to get dressed."

He goes through the living room and up some stairs. In a minute I hear voices. He's saying, "Sorry, but I have to talk to him. He's my kid. Look, you can wait in here . . ." A door closes, and I don't hear any more.

It doesn't take long for me to take off my boots and things. I leave my new jacket on the floor out of the way with the boots and step into the living room.

This might be the nicest room I've ever been in. It's got this calm peaceful feeling. The furniture is gray and pink and really clean-looking. I look for somewhere else to sit, but it's all the same, the couch and two chairs. So I pick a chair and sink back into it and it is like being on a cloud, it's so comfortable. There's a coffee table with newspapers and the TV Guide on it. There's this big cabinet thing that looks like it might hide a TV — and maybe a video game system and VCR stuff too. I wouldn't have opened it anyway, but I don't get the chance. Ryan Carroll comes back.

He's dressed now, in clean jeans and a black sweatshirt, and there's someone with him. Her hair is in a bunch of tiny braids with beads and she's wearing a sweatshirt and jeans too. Her sweatshirt is bright turquoise. She looks like she is waiting for something. She looks at Ryan Carroll and so do I.

"Gillian, this is Mitch MacLeod. Mitch, Gillian Tessier."

Gillian Tessier puts out her hand, so I walk over and shake it. She smells like heaven. And her eyes are like brown velvet. She says, "It's a pleasure to meet you, Mitch," like she means it. She talks in this nice even voice, just like she was talking to another grown-up. For some reason I can't get my tongue to work before she says, "I've got to go now, but I hope I'll see you again."

Then she puts on her ski jacket and boots and leaves P.D.Q., and I'm staring after her like a dumb thing. Ryan Carroll says, "I need some coffee. Come on out to the kitchen."

Everything is so big. The living room is bigger than Grandma and Grandpa's, and his kitchen must be as big as our living room. It's full of light-colored wood and blue and white tile. There are two big windows full of green plants. Grandma would love this, and I almost say so, before I remember where I am.

We sit at the table. There are French doors near it, so it's like sitting in the snow, but warm. Ryan Carroll drinks coffee and hands me a glass of orange juice. For ages no one says anything. Then he says, "You look so much like my sister. And like my nephew too. You all have the same eyes and hair. It's uncanny. Of course, you have your mother in you too." He says this like there is a silent "unfortunately" after it. "I'm glad you came, Mitch, but why are you here? I mean, is there any special reason?"

The more I know grownups, the dumber they seem. It's like the higher the age, the lower the IQ.

I say, "So you really are my father?"

He sits there like he hasn't a care in the world and calmly says, "Yes."

I want to hit him.

"Why didn't you come to us? Don't you think we should know each other? Don't you *want* to know me?"

As soon as that's out of my mouth, I'm

sorry. I want to take it back. My voice actually squeaked. And what if he says he doesn't? Then what? I wish I could beam over to my own kitchen and leave this place and never see him again, or hear what he has to say. But I'm not in our tiny kitchenette that looks right over the back stairs to the driveway. I'm in this wide, peaceful room with a stranger.

Ryan Carroll stops looking so calm. He frowns.

"Of course I want to know you."

I slump back in the chair. I can breathe again. It's like a huge wave washes through me. I still wouldn't mind hitting him, but I don't *have* to.

He says, "I didn't think your mother would want me around."

Well, that's true.

"Yeah, she calls you the Creep." How does he like *that*?

"She's right, I *was* a creep. A total creep. I ran scared."

! ! ! !

"So you *didn't* want to know us?"

"No, at first I didn't. I was scared to death." He starts picking at a paper serviette in a holder on the table. "Then when I finally got around to going to see your mother, she told me to get lost. She was wild. I thought if I didn't get out of there, she'd throw me out. And who could blame her?"

"What, so you never went back? You tried once in eleven years?" I'm acting mad at him, pouring scorn into my voice, but I'm wondering about my mother. She never told me about that visit.

"Yeah, pitiful, eh? So now what? Does your mother know you're here?"

"No." I get up from the table. Suddenly I feel depressed. Grown-ups are pathetic. "I'm going home."

He doesn't try to talk me out of it. Just says good-bye, as though everything is normal. Which nothing is anymore. Nothing.

17.

There's almost a week of holidays left, but so what? There's nothing to do but watch TV and play Game Boy. Megan phones once and asks me if I want to go cross-country skiing. We went once before, and it was okay. She doesn't talk a lot, Megan. She lets you think your thoughts. And when she does talk, it isn't all questions. But I don't feel like it. I don't feel like doing anything, really. Maybe I'm getting the flu. My stomach feels bad.

I watch MuchMusic and draw a lot. I especially like this one video. I feel exactly like the kids in the video even though my problem is the exact opposite: my parents aren't splitting up. They never even got together. The video shows these kids dividing in two, one walking with the mother and the other with the father.

Mum doesn't try to tell me things are wonderful, but she is *act*ing like there's no problem. Sometimes I hate everything and everyone too, just like the kids in the video.

Thursday night Mum puts her hand on my forehead.

"No fever. Headache? Hurt anywhere?"

I shake her off. "I'm okay."

She doesn't look convinced, but she lets it go. Dan is over. The Discovery Channel has a special on lions. The lionesses do all the work. They do all the hunting, but the lion takes the best food. The lionesses raise all the cubs together. When a lion comes along he might kill the cubs if he doesn't think they're his. What a depressing life.

"I'm tired. I'm going to bed."

Dan and Mum look amazed. Their mouths actually hang open. Usually I don't go to bed until they send me.

While I'm brushing my teeth, the phone rings. Usually I ignore the phone. It's never for me. But something makes me listen. After my mother answers it there's this dead silence. Then she sort of spits out, "You've got some nerve, after all this time. Go jump in the lake!" She hangs up with a crash!

Dan asks her about it, but Mum barks at him and he stops. Well, I figure I know who just got hung up on. My stomach is knotted up so tight I almost want to bend over. But my mind is clear as crystal. Will Mum tell me about this or not?

To give her a chance, I wander back to the living room. They're sitting stiffly on the couch, not touching, staring at the TV, but I bet they aren't really watching.

"Who was on the phone?" I make my voice casual.

"Wrong number," Mum says shortly. Dan doesn't look at me.

While I'm lying in bed in the dark I can't get over how you can think you know a person, but you can be completely wrong.

She lied to me.

The rest of the holiday goes by somehow. Once they drag me out tobogganing. It's no fun. I don't feel like lugging the sled back up the hill; I just want to lie in the snow until they let me go home. So I lie there and some kid walks on me! I'm disgusted. I say I'm going home. Mum tries to stop me, but Dan says, "Oh, let him go." He sounds disgusted too.

On New Year's Eve Grandma comes up to stay with me. Mum and Dan are going to a party and they don't know when they'll be home. Grandma wouldn't mind going to a party herself, but Grandpa won't go and she figures she should be with him at the beginning of the New Year. I don't know how she can stand him, but I am old enough to know not to say that. To make small talk I say, "Is he watching the game?" For some reason this strikes her as funny. She gets the giggles. She says there is no game tonight, but tomorrow will be the Rose Bowl. Well, how was I to know? Every other night seems to have a game. Anyway, forget Grandpa.

I get out the cards and we play Crazy Eights and eat popcorn. Grandma lets me pick the music so we listen to my favorite singer. Grandma says it's very catchy music. Things feel better with Grandma. She's just the same as usual. Later on we watch the Discovery Channel and she crochets. She's making these little red and white things that look like baby booties, except they'd have to be for quite a big baby. There are two already made and she's starting another one. A big three-legged baby? I pick up the finished ones.

"Grandma, these booties aren't the same size."

"Well, dear, there are going to be two sizes. One size for the woods, one for the irons."

Pardon?

"They're for Grandpa's golf clubs."

I have to laugh, and Grandma does too when I tell her what I was thinking.

We decide not to see the New Year in. She goes back to her apartment, leaving the door at the top of the stairs and the door to their living room open. And she insists on turning on the old baby monitor in case I need her. I didn't even know we still had it, but there it is in the linen cupboard on the top shelf.

I'm eleven! I'm not going to call for my grandma through a baby monitor! But it will make her feel better so I don't argue.

Tomorrow is a New Year. Big deal.

18.

For the first couple of weeks, school is just the same old same old. Then one day when I'm leaving school I have to go back to the classroom for my math book, and my luck changes. Philip gets in trouble — no surprise there — but this time it's for something he didn't do. And no one knows he's innocent except me.

It happens when I'm going through the hall on my way home for the second time. Most kids are gone already. There are two big kids outside one of the big plate-glass windows. Philip is lurking in the hall, probably looking for trouble. And does he find it. All of a sudden the big window shatters with this huge smashing sound. The sound is TERRIFIC. All this glass falls on the floor. Philip and I stare at it and then we stare at each other. His mouth is open. Maybe mine is too.

Suddenly, teachers are everywhere. They seem to come out of the woodwork. Mrs. Obadi gets there first and as soon as she knows no one got hurt she looks suspiciously at Philip. He is standing right beside the window. And as soon as she starts glaring at him he starts to look guilty. Which is weird because he didn't do anything. When the window broke he was over by the wall.

He says he didn't do anything, but the teachers don't believe him. No wonder. It's only a week since he got caught red-handed with the principal's fountain pen, and he denied that too. He catches sight of me, but before he can get them to ask me what happened, I take off. I have to think. This situation seems full of possibilities. Here's Philip Mahavolich, school bully and all-round lousy person, actually being accused of something he didn't do, and I'm the only one who knows it.

It's no surprise when the phone rings that night and it's for me. I ignore Mum's curious look.

"It's Philip," says the voice on the phone.

"What do you want?"

"The school thinks I broke that window.

They're going to suspend me! My parents are going to kill me! Tell them I didn't do it, Midget."

"Why should I?"

"Because it's the truth!"

"So? Why should I help you?"

Then Philip gets mad and swears, so I hang up and go back to doing my homework.

"Who was that?" asks Mum.

"Wrong number."

"A wrong number that asked for you."

"A coincidence. He wanted some other Mitch," I say in this tone of voice that my mother hates. She glares, but gives up.

When he phones again, I answer it.

"What is it?" I say like I'm bored.

"Midget, you gotta tell them. Come on."

"Why should I help you? What will you do for me?" There. I've made it easy for him.

"What do you want?" he whines.

"*Ev*erything. You name it, I want it. You have to do whatever I say. You have to be *nice* to me, Philip. If you're not I'll tell the principal that you bullied me into lying for you."

Silence. Finally, "For how long?"

"Forever."

This time the silence goes on for so long

that I'm just thinking he must have hung up when he says, "Okay . . . You'll tell them tomorrow?"

"Yup."

Then he does hang up.

Yes! I want to shout. Do a dance. Whirl my mother around the room. I don't, though. I just go back to the kitchen table. It's hard to think about fractions because of all the beautiful visions dancing through my head.

It works too. The next day I tell the principal Philip didn't touch the window, and she believes me. Philip doesn't say a single mean thing. I drop my pencil and he picks it up. At recess I say he has to help me in tag, just to see if he will, and he does. He starts to bug Maria so I tap him on the shoulder and shake my head. He stops. In fact, he is quiet all day. If he can't say anything mean, he doesn't seem to have much to say at all.

After a week, people are noticing. Maria and some of the other kids start coming out of their shells. Ms. Murphy compliments Philip on turning over a new leaf!

If he gets tempted and starts hassling anyone, or if I hear the beginning of "Wah! Wah!" all I have to do is sing a bit of that song, "Salvation," with slightly different words. My version goes, "Suspended, suspended, suspended are you . . ." and he pipes down. It's a miracle.

19.

School is a whole different world since I've got Philip in my power.

Home isn't, though. For one thing, I'm still avoiding the Eccles because of that soother incident. Since Mrs. Eccles always seems to be out with the carriage, except on weekends when Mr. Eccles is out with it, I try not to hang around outside.

Inside is even worse. My mother is a stranger. I don't believe Mum now when she tells me things. She gets mad one day when I lie about where I was after school. I don't know why I lied. I haven't gone near the Creep's since the holidays, and I wasn't doing anything wrong. I went to the library, for Pete's sake! But I say I went to Dan's garage, and then she asks him and he says I wasn't there and she goes spare.

But I don't care. I yell, "You should talk about lying! Who phoned you again last night and you hung up again! Was it *another* wrong number?"

She turns white. My mother prides herself on her honesty and I used to too, but how can I? How can she live with herself? I don't even know her anymore.

Then Dan tells me to watch my mouth. Dan, who has never ever told me off before!

"You can't boss me around! You're not my father!" I slam the door to my room. I don't know why I said that either, except I really do not want Dan to start bossing me around. But I wouldn't let the Creep boss me around, either. Why does he phone her? Why doesn't he just come around and *make* her talk to him? Why didn't he do that a long time ago?

In February it rains and thaws and finally gets cold and snows again. Mum and Dan drag me out tobogganing. We've kind of declared a truce. As far as I know, there haven't been any more phone calls. I am trying not to lie too much, at least about important stuff. Dan hasn't tried to boss me around again. Mum is being extra-nice and extra-patient. It's sickening, but better than fighting, I guess.

It's not that cold and the hill is fast today. It's a sunny-cloudy day. Blue sky and white clouds. I've been feeling crummy today, probably fighting a flu bug, but Mum was right: the fresh air does seem to be helping.

Mum waits on the sled while Dan and I get on the toboggan. Down at the foot of the hill, a car pulls up on the street. More tobogganers, likely. We won't have the hill to ourselves for long. Dan and I finally get settled. We're ready to race. Hope these new people stay out of the way. Little kids can be real speed bumps!

I yell, "One-two-THREE!" and we push off. Mum shoots ahead at the start, but on the hill we gain on her. Not enough, though. She sails all the way to the fence.

Just as we're getting off the toboggan and sled I notice that the person getting out of the car isn't dressed for tobogganing. This tall man in a topcoat and shiny shoes is crossing the snow toward Mum. It's Ryan Carroll!

Oh boy. Just for a split second no one but me knows who he is. Then Mum realizes. She's reaching for her sled's rope and there's a little pause when it hits her. Then she grabs it and starts walking toward the hill, fast. But fast for Mum isn't that fast for him. He's much taller. He keeps up easily and Mum is getting steamed.

Dan's like, "What's going on?" but no one answers him.

Ryan Carroll says, "Tiffany, stop and talk to me."

"Buzz off!"

"I'll just keep coming back. You may as well get it over with." Now they're starting up the hill. I'm tagging along so I don't miss anything. She marches up with her eyes straight ahead; he keeps beside her. Finally she wheels around ahead of him, so he has to take a step back. Because of the hill they're eye to eye.

"Get lost or I'll charge you with harassment!"

Dan chugs up to them. "Hey, who are you? Leave her alone!"

Ryan Carroll stands there with his hands beside him. "Just talk to me, Tiffany."

Now here comes Gillian Tessier, slogging through the snow in high heels! No one but me seems to notice.

Mum says, "Give me one good reason why I should talk to you."

Then everyone talks at once.

"Mitch came to see me," says Ryan Carroll.

"Beat it, buddy. Last chance," says Dan.

"Ms. MacLeod, you are upsetting your son," says Gillian Tessier.

"Keep out of this, Gillian," snaps Ryan Carroll.

"Butt out, Dan!" says Mum.

And then there is silence. In the whole white sweep of playground nothing moves for one, two, three beats. Until everyone speaks at once again.

"Fine, I'll wait in the car," huffs Gillian Tessier.

"Mind if I walk with you?" asks Dan.

"Okay, talk," says Mum.

"Thanks," says Ryan Carroll.

"Mum, listen to him!" That's me.

She says, "Mitch!" as though she had forgotten I was there. "Oh, Mitch. Meet me at home, eh? Here, get yourself a chocolate bar or something." She digs a toonie out of her jeans.

And that's how I leave them: Dan and Gillian Tessier sitting in the flash red car, my mother and Ryan Carroll standing face to face on the hill.

20.

When Dan and Mum come home, they are arguing. Dan is mad because he didn't know who Ryan Carroll was and Mum is accusing him of being jealous. As soon as they get in, Mum says we have to clean the place up. It seems Ryan Carroll and Gillian Tessier were on their way to a wedding. They will be coming here right after the service, and Ryan Carroll and Mum will talk.

Mum flies around, picking things up off the couch and floor. She shoves my Game Boy and a bunch of other stuff at me to take to my room. Then she goes out to clean up the kitchen while I vacuum the living room. Dan stands in the middle of it all.

"So what are Mitch and I supposed to do while you and Brad Pitt are having this Summit?"

Ooh boy, he *must* be jealous! But Mum ignores him. We've barely finished cleaning up when the doorbell rings. I go down the inside stairs. Right beside our outside door is the door to Grandma and Grandpa's living room, which is always kept closed. I can hear the game on TV. It's such an ordinary sound on this extraordinary day.

Ryan Carroll and Gillian Tessier are super dressed up. I didn't notice on the playground. When I get them upstairs we all stand around in the hall for a minute while introductions are made. Dan and Ryan Carroll shake hands and say, "Good to meet you," but for once Dan isn't full of jokes. He just stares at Ryan Carroll like he's lost his light saber and now here's Darth Vader come to call.

Mum and Gillian Tessier shake hands too, and say hello politely. No one talks to me. Then everyone sits in the living room. Mum says I'll bring coffee in a few minutes. This is news to me! And they do what grown-ups do. They "make small talk" about what no one is thinking about. Mum asks about the wedding and Gillian Tessier answers. Ryan Carroll talks a bit. Only Dan doesn't open his mouth.

Our living room feels full. I'm on a kitchen

chair I've dragged in. Mum is in the La-Z-Boy and Dan and Ryan Carroll and Gillian Tessier are lined up on the couch.

It is weird. Our house is clean, I know that. Mum and I clean it every weekend. But it doesn't really look it. It looks dingy. The coffee table is chipped and scratched. And nothing looks new, that's for sure.

Plus, Ryan Carroll and Gillian Tessier are so elegant, they make everyone else look ordinary.

Dan gets up. He stands very straight and he's sucking his stomach in so hard that when he talks it sounds like he's grunting. He grunts that he'll get the coffee.

"Are you all right, Dan?" asks Mum, frowning.

He glares at her and grunts, "Sure." I follow him.

In the kitchen he doesn't say anything. Just pours four cups of coffee and points at the small tray with cream and sugar on it, so I pick it up. I can always get my own Coke later, since it seems I've been completely forgotten. He picks up the bigger tray with the cups on it and leads the way.

When we come back, Mum is saying soon

we'll be having a wedding too. No date set yet, but they hope this June. (This is news to me!) Ryan Carroll and Gillian Tessier say congratulations to Dan. Ryan Carroll half stands up to shake his hand. Dan stops sucking in his stomach. It sags out so fast there's a little whoosh, and he smiles for the first time all afternoon.

Gillian Tessier stands up. "I won't stay for coffee. You must have a lot to talk about. Ryan, I'll see you at the reception, okay?" He hands her his keys. Dan says he'll be going too, and asks me if I want to come, but no way I'm missing this! He kisses Mum and shakes Ryan Carroll's hand quite enthusiastically before he goes. Finally I am alone with my father and mother.

At first no one says anything. Then Ryan Carroll says he likes our living room. He says all the pictures make it feel homey. My mother says it's been great having Grandma just downstairs. Then it gets awkward and Mum asks me to leave.

"We have a lot to talk about, Mitch. If you're worried about not getting to talk to your father, maybe you guys could set a time to get together."

Ryan Carroll says, "What about tomorrow

afternoon?" so I say okay. Then I leave, but once they think I'm in my room I go to the bathroom and from there I sneak into the kitchen. Squeezed between the fridge and the table and leaning against the wall, I can hear perfectly.

"You must hate me," says Ryan Carroll. That's the last I hear of *his* voice for awhile. Mum starts to talk and boy does she tell him off. Right away I'm learning things. Like I had no idea it was so awful giving birth. She always says, "I wouldn't go through it for anyone but you, Mitch buddy." But it sounds like it was dangerous. Sixteen doesn't sound young to me, but it's young for having babies. That's what she's telling him. Then she starts giving him gross details about how long we were in the hospital and stuff. I plug my ears!

When I unplug them she's onto crying. She's talking so fast I miss parts, but I can hear enough to know she is not painting a pretty picture of babyhood. Apparently it is possible for a human to survive on three hours sleep a night for months on end. She talks about sleep for a long time. She mentions sick babies, teething babies, fevers of 104 degrees. She talks as though I was all these difficult babies. She talks for quite awhile about some baby from hell — her words! — who cried for twenty-two out of twenty-four hours.

I have her word for it that I was a great baby although I had colic, which is a stomach-ache that babies get sometimes. I used to like to be rocked, so she and Grandma took turns in the rocking chair. They practically rocked a groove in the floor; that's how much they liked me. So she's not being exactly honest with my father, talking about these difficult babies as though I was like that too. I don't know about Ryan Carroll, but *I'm* bored.

Then she's onto money. He tries to say something but she talks over him. "No, I don't want your money."

Finally she winds down. She finishes up with, "You were a real rat."

He says, "I know." There's a long pause. Then he says he was scared of his parents.

"*You* were scared. Geez, have you met my father? He thinks I am the original scarlet woman. And he's horrible to Mitch. If it hadn't been for my mother I might have jumped off a cliff, I mean it. And there you were finishing school, cool as you please, making the Honors List, going to university. Like a rat off a sinking ship."

"You're right. I walked. I just wish you could have walked too. Wouldn't you have walked, if you could?"

There's this silence. Then my mother laughs. She laughs and laughs. Once she's started, she can't seem to stop. Finally she winds down. She says, "You know it, Carroll."

For a while no one talks. Then Ryan Carroll says, "I'm really sorry, Tiffany. I was a real jerk."

Mum says, "You'd better not hurt Mitch. I mean it."

"I won't! He's a great kid. I like him. You've done a great job with him."

Ahem! I think my ears are burning. But not for long. My own mother betrays me.

"He *is* a great kid, but he can also be a pain in the neck. He lies, and he can be mouthy. What if you get tired of him? He won't always be on his best behavior with you. Then what?"

How can she say these awful things about me? Her own son! She's totally scaring him off.

"We'll take it slowly. I'm in for the duration, though. I mean it."

"I hope so. You mess that kid around and I don't know what I'll do, but you won't like it."

"I hear you."

It's amazing she hasn't scared him off! He leaves then, but they are going to meet again next weekend to "sort things out." And tomorrow I am going to Ryan Carroll's house for the first time without lying.

21.

This time when I go to Ryan Carroll's house it's different: he knows I'm coming. But I'm kind of nervous anyway. I don't know why. He smiles when he answers the door and takes my coat and shows me where to hang it up next time. Next time!

Then he says he is just finishing up some work and would I mind playing video games by myself for a while? Mind? Of course I don't mind! It turns out he has an old system, Nintendo 64, and the game in it is Mario Kart. I was hoping for PlayStation 2. The Campbell-McAllisters have N64, so I have played it a few times, but they didn't have Mario Kart, so I fool around finding out how it works. By the time Ryan Carroll comes back the steering is no problem and I've raced a couple of G.P.s.

He sits down and picks up the other controller.

"You ever played Mario Kart before?"

"No."

"Let me show you some tricks." So he shows me how to do slide turns and how to make really fast starts. Then he shows me a short cut at Koopa Troopa Beach. There's a hole in a rock and once I see it I get through it on my second try. We play all afternoon except when we take a break to get a drink. I'm hoping for Coke but it's juice. He has orange-grapefruit, though, which I like. Anyway, I can't believe how fast the afternoon goes. It's dark out. I check my watch and say I better go home, we're going to Grandma's for dinner.

He asks if I want a ride home. In that flash car! Naturally I say sure. I ask him all about it. He hasn't had it very long, but he says it's the kind that's supposed to last a lifetime. I bet Dan would love to see under the hood, but I stop myself just in time from saying it.

He lets me out at the driveway. I wonder if I should ask him in. Would he come? Would Mum like that? But there's no chance. He waves and drives off.

Uh-oh, while I've been standing here the

Eccles have walked up, pushing Jennifer who is crying, surprise-surprise! "Hi, Mitch," they both say, so I can't pretend not to see them. I can't look them in the eye. They must think I'm the lowest of the low, stealing a pacifier from a baby.

They don't say anything about it. In fact, they don't act any different than they used to. Right away they're telling me about why Jennifer is crying. Apparently she's teething. They always say she's teething. She must have more teeth than an Edmontosaurus, which my book says it would take a dentist a week to clean. She doesn't even look at me, either. Maybe she doesn't recognize me anymore.

Then Mr. Eccles turns serious. "Mitch, I've been hoping to run into you. That boy who came to the street party last fall, is he a friend of yours?"

"No way!"

"Good, I'm glad to hear it. You can do better than that. That wasn't a very nice trick he played, and then blaming it on you."

"You *know*?" I've been skulking and hiding all winter for nothing?

"Yes, I know. I didn't believe him when he blamed you because it was so out of character for you. And then it turned out Mrs. Sloan saw him."

"Let's go, Jonathan. Jennifer needs her dinner." Mrs. Eccles moves off with the carriage.

"Bye, Mitch!" Mr. Eccles hurries after her with the shopping. I stand there stunned.

Well, what do you know? Not everyone is taken in by Philip. They knew I wouldn't take the pacifier.

Grandma has made this huge feast: chili, potatoes, cauliflower with cheese sauce, salad, apple pie. Grandpa asks what I've been up to this afternoon, and I almost lie from habit, but I catch myself.

I'm not going to lie. But what should I say? I don't know what to call Ryan Carroll. "My father" still sounds strange. "Dad" is out of the question! He hasn't said I can call him "Ryan," but "Mr. Carroll" doesn't seem right for my own father. So I say, "I've been to Ryan Carroll's house."

Grandpa says, "Oh, is that a school friend?"

There's this silence at the table. I look at Mum, but she is eating without looking at anyone. Grandma smiles at me, so I say firmly, "Ryan Carroll is my father."

Grandpa puts down his knife and fork. "I

don't understand," he says. "Tiffany?"

"Yes?"

"Mitchell has just said he was visiting his father. How is that possible?"

"He only lives over on Mary Street," I say. Everyone ignores me.

Now Grandpa looks at Grandma. She nods.

This is pretty weird; there's this big thing hanging in the air, but I'm not sure what it is. Grandpa looks like he's seen a ghost. He also looks like he might get mad any minute. I'm finished my dinner, so I excuse myself and go home. Any fight with Grandpa is bound to be worth missing.

22.

And that's how it goes. Every weekend I go over to Ryan Carroll's house. We switch to Saturdays because Mum is usually working, and I usually have dinner at his house before he drives me home. Unless he's going out for dinner.

He's into health foods, it turns out. He's very interested that we are vegetarians. He has wondered about becoming vegetarian himself, but so far he's just buying free-range eggs and chickens. He also buys organic vegetables, which sometimes have bugs in them. Gross, but he says, "At least the bugs wash off." He makes this salad with goat's cheese, which is disgusting. And there is yogurt with every meal. Plain yogurt, not fruit yogurt. There's one good thing, though: this terrific spaghetti sauce that has no tomatoes in it, just peanut butter and tahini, which is ground-up sesame seeds. It is fantastic and actually goes great with the yogurt.

He never buys fast food or ordinary snacks. No chocolate bars! No chips! No pop! In fact, according to him all that stuff is terrible for children.

"Empty calories, Mitch. They take up room so you don't get enough of the calories that help you grow. And Coke is terrible for kids, worse than other pop. It has caffeine in it, which is addictive, for one thing, and it sucks the calcium from your bones. Now they want to put caffeine in other pop too, like they do in the States. It's a terrible idea. Getting kids addicted to something that's bad for them. You should drink milk or juice. Tell me your favorite juice and I'll get some."

Sometimes I go grocery shopping with him, if he hasn't had a chance to do it before I get there. Grocery shopping is something I usually avoid like the plague. If we run out of Dipps or medium cheddar or something, I just put it on the list and Mum gets it on her day off, which is usually Monday.

Ryan Carroll's usual shopping day is Saturday. He whizzes right past whole aisles, like the one with pickles and Cheez Whiz.

"Read the label," he says when I mention Cheez Whiz. I don't know what he means. I *did* read the label: it says CHEEZ WHIZ. Duh. But I try to be patient. It turns out he means the list of ingredients, which is in tiny print. It is a really long list.

"That's all food additives."

We move on to the dairy section where he hands me some whipping cream.

"Read the ingredients."

I do. I can't find any cream. All it says is "milk ingredients, dextrose, carrageenan, mono and diglycerides, cellulose gum, polysorbate 80, sodium citrate."

"It's disgusting. Why do you read all this?" I ask him.

"For a while I had to. I was allergic to a lot of additives so I had to avoid them for a whole year. Now I'm over it, but I can't forget it."

Well, I intend to read labels as little as possible. It might put me right off my food.

Naturally, Ryan Carroll also believes in keeping fit and building muscles. He works out in a gym. He says I can come too, if I want. No thanks! One day he offers to put a fitness video on and get out his smallest weights for me. By that time I'm more used to being there so I speak up. "Why would I want to do that?"

"To get strong and healthy."

"I'm already healthy. I don't come here to exercise. Exercise is boring."

"Oh." By the look on his face I figure he's remembering my mother saying I'm mouthy. But geez, just because he likes to work out doesn't mean I have to. I'm his son, not his clone.

But speaking of fitness and bodies and things . . . "Were you small when you were my age?"

Ryan Carroll thinks. He puts on a tactful face so it must be bad news.

"I wasn't the smallest, but I was smaller than average," he says.

Well, that's not *so* bad.

"When did you grow?"

"Grade Nine."

Another two and a half years.

"My brother didn't grow until grade eleven, though."

"Grade eleven!" It comes out as a wail.

"He was a real shrimp until then. Then he

grew six inches in one year. Now he's taller than I am."

My father and my uncle (Another uncle! Will I meet him? Does he know about me?) are both tall. Late-growing, but tall.

When I'm over and Ryan Carroll is busy on his computer or making dinner I usually play Nintendo. One day, though, I feel like drawing, so I turn on MuchMusic and ask for some paper. He's cutting vegetables.

"There's some in the desk. I'll get it, I'm not sure which drawer."

He wipes his hands and we head down the hall to his study. As we pass the living room he stops dead. Then he goes into the living room and takes one look at the TV and turns it off. It was showing this super-gross video where a guy's skin is peeled off. I can't watch it, it is sick-making.

"Mitch, you're too young for MuchMusic."

I shrug.

"Do you watch it at home?"

I shrug again. He frowns.

"Well, not here, okay? They show stuff no other station gets away with until after nine. Like that. Okay?"

I say okay, no problem. Most videos are

not like that one, though. There's a lot more stuff that isn't okay in this house than I'm used to, if you count all the health food rules.

"Come help me make the salad. You can pick the music."

He has a CD player in the kitchen and he even has the new CD by my favorite singer, so we listen to that.

Even though I'm going over every week, it's awhile before I know what to call him. Finally I ask.

He says, "What would you like to call me?"

Uh-uh. I'm not going first.

"Whatever you want," I say.

"What do you call Dan?"

"Dan."

"Well, you could call me Ryan. Or, you could call me Dad."

"What do *you* want?" I ask.

"Well, everyone calls me Ryan. It would be nice if you called me Dad."

YES! I am *so* glad! But I'm cool. "Okay, I'll try."

I don't see Gillian Tessier again for ages, but I know Ryan — Dad — does. Usually he's on his way to see her when he drops me off. Sometimes he takes a shower and gets all dressed up and smells nice before we go. They go to plays and concerts. He's going to take me to a play some time.

It turns out he sees Mum too. This is how I find out:

Dan comes over one Friday with Indian take-out. Mum is moaning about her feet. She has taken off her shoes and put her feet on the coffee table.

While Dan's setting out the food he says, "Guess who came by the garage today. Your father, Mitch. And he's selling his Beemer!"

What on earth is a Beemer? It sounds like a method of transport used in "Star Trek."

"Yeah, he said he was going to stop by," says Mum, hobbling over to the table. I help myself to the onion bhajis.

"When did you see him?" asks Dan, quick as a flash. His voice is sharp, but he sits back, trying to look casual. The beadiness of his eyes gives him away, big time.

"We had lunch yesterday."

Dan frowns. He starts arranging things on the table, putting serving spoons around and then picking them up again. His fingers are jerky. I can read his mind like a book. He doesn't want to say anything in case he sounds jealous, which he would. Mum goes on, while she helps herself and passes dishes to me.

"We talked money. He's convinced me. He and Chris are going to work out an agreement for support, and he's going to give me a lump sum to start with. That's probably why he's selling his car."

Selling his car?! This is news. That flash red car. There must be some mistake.

"I thought you didn't want his money," Dan says in this accusing voice. "He'll get a fortune for the Beemer. It's only a year old and they don't depreciate."

"Oh, really?" Mum doesn't sound that interested. She doesn't care about cars, but she does care about Dan. Doesn't she see how fidgety he is? She's busy loading up her plate. "Pass the rice, please, Mitch. He hasn't paid for it yet, you know. Most of what he gets will go to pay off the bank loan. And he's right, he owes me. God knows I could use it. We could use it." Mum squeezes Dan's arm, but he doesn't look happy.

"We're doing all right," he says. "I've got some savings . . ."

"But I don't. Not a penny. And I'm only twenty-seven, but my feet hurt. Geez, I don't want to be a hairdresser forever. I'm not cut out for it."

Nyuk! Nyuk! Not cut out for being a hairdresser! Usually Mum would notice and laugh, but she barrels right on.

"Ryan's going to pay for me to get trained in something else. That's what the cash is for. Things might be tight for awhile, Dan, before I get working again, but I'd really like to do it. I'm thinking of something with computers. That's where the jobs are."

Dan doesn't say anything so Mum says, "Would you really rather I didn't take anything from him?"

"Of course, I'd rather. Wouldn't you?"

"It's fair, Dan. He's Mitch's father. He wants to get to know him and help pay to bring him up. He knows I'd be trained in something else by now like he is if things had been different."

She means if she didn't have me. Dan ignores it all.

"Would you really say no if I asked you to?"

"I don't know."

Dan starts talking about supporting Mum and me, but he doesn't get far before Mum says "Yuck! I'll support myself, thank you very much."

Dan gets huffy. Mum puts her hand on his arm.

"Come on, Dan, I know he's a bit of a clotheshorse, but he wants to do the right thing."

Finally Dan smiles, and even chuckles a bit. "He is, isn't he?"

"What's a clotheshorse?" I ask.

"Oh, nothing bad, Mitch," says Mum, remembering I'm there. "Just someone who likes new clothes and things."

They aren't mad, anyway. I can tell they will be talking for ages, so I excuse myself. I find my book and go read on my bed.

23.

Grandma is nowhere to be found. I'm supposed to ask her if she's going to be home tonight. Mum and Dan want to go out to a movie and they like someone to be in the house, and *I* like that someone to be Grandma. I check the living room. Grandpa is sitting there alone so I back out, but he calls me back. There's an amazing thing — the TV isn't on.

"Isn't the game on?" I ask, when he doesn't say anything. They get The Sports Network so Grandma always says Grandpa's in heaven twenty-four/seven. In fact, she doubts their TV gets any other channel. TSN has worn a groove along their cable, she figures, so nothing else can get through. So why is there no game?

"Mitchell," he says and then stops.

I wait. Finally he seems to make up his mind. "You're a good boy. I'm sorry if I've been hard on you. This is for you." And he hands me a red bill.

It must be fake, or play money, or foreign. I've seen green, blue, purple money, and even an old orange two-dollar bill, but never red. The number on it is "fifty."

"Is this real?"

"Yes, it is. It isn't counterfeit; I got it at the bank."

Fifty dollars! I'm so busy gawking at it I haven't even thanked him.

"Thanks! Really, Grandpa, thanks a million!"

"That's all right. Maybe sometime we can play chess if you like. Now away you go."

It is unbelievable. Grandpa must have had a personality transplant.

It's like it won't be real until I show someone. I take the steps two at a time and charge into the kitchen. Mum's just serving up. Dan's already at the table.

"Look what Grandpa gave me!" I wave the bill in the air. Mum and Dan take one look at it, and then they look at each other. Finally they look at me.

Mum smiles. "Wow! Lucky you. Any ideas how you want to spend it?"

"A million." I'm washing my hands at the sink.

"You better put that away before it blows behind the stove or something."

So I go to my room and put it in my wallet in my desk. I have never played any game with Grandpa just the two of us, even though he really likes chess. When I asked he always said I was too young. And he has never given me a present before. On my birthday and Christmas there's always something from him and Grandma, but it's clothes that Grandma has bought after asking Mum what I need. It's all I can think of over supper. Great as it is, I do wonder a bit why.

"Maybe he's had a change of heart. About time," says Mum.

Suddenly I'm struck with an awful thought: my mother needs money for a new pair of shoes for work. She said so last night. I figure I should offer her the money, but I just can't. Instead I say, "Mum, do you need some money? We could share it."

Mum's face scrunches up. Her eyes get bright, but no wonder the way she's pinching her nose so hard.

"Oh, Mitch," she says with her mouth all twisted funny. "Thanks. But no. It's yours. All yours." She smiles then, a watery smile, and I wonder why she seems about to cry. Should I ask? No, she's better now.

I'm excused from dishes so I take off to phone Daniel. I ask him about video games. This is my chance to buy one. He's got a new one for his Game Boy and he says he'll bring it to school tomorrow so I can try it.

24.

Daniel's right. It's a good game. The only question is, should I get it or should I maybe get another good game and we could trade sometimes?

Philip looms up while we're discussing this. I'm just about to tell him to buzz off when he holds out a connector cord.

"Want to use this? I brought it to use with Richard, but he forgot to bring his Game Boy."

"Sure! Thanks!"

He doesn't go away, either. Turns out his brothers have a bunch of Game Boy games so we ask him about which ones are good. When I tell him I've got enough money to buy one he turns green with envy.

Then in school an incredible thing happens. We have been writing stories all week. Yesterday we copied out the final draft and handed it in. Now Ms. Murphy gives them back and asks for volunteers to read them. Of course I don't put up my hand; reading goes like a charm for me most of the time at home and with Ms. Petrillo, but I have still never managed to read out loud in class. Never — in seven years of school.

I wrote about this cartoonist whose drawings come to life and start appearing everywhere he goes. Daniel knows what my story is about. Also I have told him that I read at home. So Daniel betrays me — he puts up his hand and asks for my story!

Ms. Murphy asks me if I will read it. I look down at the top page. The title is "Inky Scribbler and the Magic Paper." The first sentence sits there and looks clear and calm: "One day Inky Scribbler ran out of his usual drawing paper. In desperation he borrowed some parcel wrap from the janitor . . ."

"Yes," I say. The whole class falls silent. I read the whole story, which is three pages long. All the words stay calm and clear. And when I know, on the second page, that they are going to keep doing that, I start to enjoy myself. I put expression into it. When I read my last line, the class cracks up and then they actually CLAP.

"Way to go, Midget," says Richard.

"Midget! Great story!" says Chevy.

"Neat ending!" says Philip. (Philip!) "Say, Midget, what happens next? Are you going to write a sequel?"

"Maybe I will," I say, liking the idea. Then I feel this rush of happiness and it makes me brave. "By the way, guys, my name is Mitch."

25.

Easter comes. I hunt for eggs before Mum and Dan are even up. They won't be up for hours because they were out late last night, dancing up a storm. They always sleep in late the next morning when they've been dancing. For breakfast I eat a bunch of malted eggs and a whole chocolate rabbit from ears to tail. Then I read for awhile. They still aren't up so I play Game Boy, and then turn on the Discovery Channel, but it's all interviews.

So I put on MuchMusic and draw for awhile. Mum has recently asked me not to watch it anymore. She said she never realized it was so violent and sexist. So I don't very much, especially when she's around. But right now there's nothing else to do. Finally I figure maybe they're sick or something and I should check on them. I go and knock on their door.

They come staggering out with their eyes half-open. Dan says, "I can't believe it's noon. Sorry, bud." Mum heads for the kitchen and fumbles over the coffee maker. It isn't until they're drinking their coffee that Mum opens her eyes wide enough to look at a clock.

"It isn't noon!" she screams. "It's only ten o'clock in the morning!"

I never said it was noon; Dan did. They grump some more and it almost looks like they're going back to bed, but we're saved by the phone. It's Grandma. She's calling about whose car to take to Easter dinner. We're going to this big restaurant, Uncle Brandon's treat. He has this tiny apartment, so whenever it's his turn to have a family dinner he takes us to a restaurant. It's great because you can have whatever you want without hurting anyone's feelings. Like if you don't eat Megan's cabbage salad or drink Grandpa's punch, they might notice. But the restaurant doesn't care what you order, or whether you eat it.

We dress up for the dinner. My best pants are the jeans I got at Christmas, and there's my button-up navy shirt. It will just be our family, but that's quite a few people: Auntie Chris and Megan, Uncle Brandon and whoever, Grandma and Grandpa, Mum and Dan, and me. I am the only one who isn't half of a pair.

This gets me thinking. I've been an only child all my life, but is it possible Mum and Dan will want a baby? They do seem to make more fuss than is strictly called for about Jennifer. Jennifer is walking now, and half the time when we come out of our house there she is with one of her parents following. She runs sort of stiff-legged with her arms up. She always looks like she's going to fall, but she usually doesn't. Dan gushes over her on our way to the car. That must be a symptom of impending parenthood: Jennifer is a very ordinary baby.

"So, are you guys thinking of having a baby?" I ask from the back seat.

Right away they look at each other, alarmed. Don't tell me this is another subject they're worried about talking to me about. I know there's this saying that love is blind, but in their case love has made them dense.

"I don't care, as long as I don't have to share my room with it or take care of it." May as well set the ground rules early.

They shrug their eyebrows at each other.

Mum says, "Well, Mitch, you never know. You just might end up with a sister or brother. Stranger things have happened."

At the restaurant we have a room to ourselves. It's just eight of us because Uncle Brandon didn't bring anyone. I order chili with blueberry pie for dessert. Everyone's in a good mood.

When dessert comes, Uncle Brandon says, "Well, everyone, I have some good news. I got the job at Nipissing. I'll be moving up there this summer."

Everyone starts congratulating him and asking questions.

"Where is Nipissing?" I say.

"In North Bay. It's a university. North Bay is about 250 miles north of here; it's just northeast of Georgian Bay."

"How many kilometers is that?"

"About four hundred. I'll show you on the map sometime. It's almost a day's drive. And Mitch, I was wondering if you'd like to come up for a couple of weeks this summer. There are two good lakes for swimming. We could go camping too. If it's okay with your Mum and Dan."

A whole two weeks with Uncle Brandon.

Swimming, camping, maybe canoeing? Yes, sure, he says, he'll rent a canoe. This sounds great.

Mum and Dan have an announcement too. They've set the date for the wedding. It's going to be at the end of June, and then they're going for a week's honeymoon. It seems to have been arranged that I'll stay with my father while they're gone. Thanks for asking me!

I wonder if Dad will have moved then or will he still be in his parents' house. They'll be coming back this summer from their sabbatical, and Dad is going to move into an apartment. It's going to have a spare room I can use to sleep over. When he told me that, I figured maybe I'd stay over one night sometime.

But maybe a whole week will be good. Things sure are going to be different.

26.

Mum's hair has almost grown the pink out. She gets it cut and boy, does she look different with brown hair. That isn't going to last, though. She's going to dye it to match her wedding dress when she gets it.

She and Auntie Chris go shopping a lot for the dress she's getting married in. It takes ages — no plain white for my mum! Finally she buys one. It's a silky material with big bright flowers splashed over a white background. The flowers are purple and pink and yellow with a bit of green.

Mum decides to dye her hair green with a purple streak, and she waits until the week before the wedding to do it so no roots will show. Even I have to admit it looks pretty good. Surprisingly good. I wonder if she could do mine like that. Maybe next September when school is starting and hers has grown out (no way I'm having matching mother-son hair!). I'll think about it before asking her. No point getting her hopes up.

Dad gets an apartment right uptown near where the new movie theatre is going to be. I can walk there no problem from home or from next year's school (grade seven!). Daniel is going to that school too, it turns out.

I hope Mum and Dan won't want to move out to the suburbs. I don't want to move out where you have to get a ride everywhere just like a little kid. Here I can walk or ride my bike everywhere I need to go. It's close to Dan's work too. I'll have to sound them out. Right now I have a lot of influence with them — for a change! — because they want me to be happy they're getting married.

Dad takes me to get furniture for my room in his apartment. He wants a double bed for it so he can use it as a guestroom when I'm not there. I get this great idea. Instead of a double bed, maybe Dad could buy bunk beds and then Daniel could sleep over sometimes. Dad really doesn't want to do that, but when I see a bunk bed where the bottom bunk is double and the top is single, he gives in. It's a compromise.

Also he gets me a desk with drawers that lock for my private stuff, and a boring chest of drawers. (Yawn, who cares whether it has four drawers or five?) I ask for a computer for my room and he says "In your dreams." We do get a bookcase and a night table, though, and a Darth Vader lamp. The light saber can be left on as a nightlight.

My feet are killing me by the time we get that far. I beg him to pick out the comforter himself.

"How about we take a break for lunch before we go to the poster store?" he says.

Now he's talking! And I'm in luck — there's no health-food place in the mall food court. It's a choice of pizza, cheese sandwich or New York Fries, which is my absolute favorite. Dad frowns. Is he going to make us leave the mall to drive somewhere that has bean sprouts?

"Chips have Vitamin C," I point out.

And just this once, he says, "Yes." With milk, but still. I love New York Fries. I eat a whole Medium by myself. Dad looks amazed. I don't often eat that much with him. I wonder why.

Now I'm ready to look at posters. The store

has so many I have to look at all of them, and then it is hard to decide. Dad says we can start with three and come back for more if I want. He isn't impatient at all. There are movie posters — lots of *Star Wars* ones. There are posters of singers. Two very good ones of my favorite singer showing her talent. There are unicorn posters, volcano posters, cartoon posters. You name it, that store probably has a poster of it.

Finally I pick one of my favorite singer dancing, one of pod racing in *Star Wars*, where the stars look like streaks, and one that is a map of the universe. Dad gets that one laminated.

My room is going to be great.

Then when my birthday comes Dad gives me the new CD I want. *And* Mum raises my allowance by like five hundred percent! I now get twelve dollars a week! There are a few strings attached — I have to save some and I have to give some to charity — but I am going to be RICH.

27.

Mum and Dan get married in a special wedding chapel that isn't a church. They wrote their own vows, referring to God as She, but otherwise pretty standard, as far as I can tell. I get to stand up with them, and so do Auntie Chris and Dan's brother from Nova Scotia. I'm wearing a *suit*. I get a good view of the audience. Dad and Gillian Tessier are there sitting with Megan right behind Grandma and Grandpa. Mum wasn't going to invite them, but Dan wanted to. Uncle Brandon and someone named Veronica are beside Grandpa. While the vows are being said Grandma wipes her eyes — no surprise there! Then *Grandpa* of the stone heart wipes *his* eyes. Wonders will never cease.

Mum and Dan look pretty happy and not

nervous at all. When it's over Mum says to everyone, "Let's party!"

And we do, at this hall they rented. There's this buffet so you can eat as much as you want, and the speeches are all kept really short. Most of them are funny too, except Grandpa's. He gets kind of heavy, talking about the "solemnity of marriage." Mum catches his eye and draws her finger across her throat so he cuts it short.

There's *lots* of dancing. Thanks to Mum I can dance anything except what kids my age do dance, but since I am practically the only kid there, that doesn't matter. I dance with everyone. First Mum, of course. It's a fast rock song.

"Let's jive, Mitch," she says, so we do, though I'm a little nervous. I've only ever done it in the garage when we practice. It's fun, though. She laughs; she's so happy. I'm laughing too, spinning her. Then I dance with Dan's mother, who asks me to call her Grandma! But luckily she doesn't wait for an answer. And soon she'll be back in Nova Scotia.

Next I dance with Auntie Chris, and then Megan. Then Gillian Tessier asks me to dance with her! I'd never have dared ask her, she's so elegant. She smells so gorgeous I actually wonder if I'm going to faint. I don't know how Dad can think straight around her. I have to sit down and drink a Coke when our dance is finally over.

Chevy comes over. She's the only other kid there. The band starts playing an Avril Lavigne song.

"Come on, Mitch," she says, pulling me to my feet. "None of this mushy old-fashioned stuff, either."

I just do what she does and it isn't bad. I go to sit down but she says, "Stay up and show me how to jive, okay?" So I do.

By the time Dad takes me to his apartment I'm so tired I don't know if I can sleep. My posters are flat on the floor so I can decide where they go. I'm going to be here a whole week. Believe it or not, I miss my mum.

My suitcase is on the bed. I dig out my pajamas and close it back up and dump it on the floor. Once I'm in the bed it feels weird not knowing what the room looks like, so I turn on the light saber nightlight, which looks pretty funny: this long pink thing glowing in the dark, fuzzy without my glasses.

The bed is really comfortable. I settle into

it, slide my feet through the cool sheets. They smell clean.

Maybe it's good I'll be here for a week.

Dad's taken the week off work so he can get settled into his new apartment. Maybe if I have him for a whole week, I can play some games on his computer. Maybe he'll buy a PlayStation 2. Maybe I can talk him into going to Pizza Hut. Maybe I can break his habit of trying to get me to exercise with him. Maybe we can watch a movie and eat chips with it! He thinks chips aren't so bad for kids, not nearly as bad as pop and other junk food. When we were at the health food store I saw a whole rack of all different flavors of chips. We could try those.

I'll wear him down, eventually.

Shelagh Lynne Supeene has always loved to read and she has always loved to write. She was already creating booklets for her parents to read when she was eight years old. Her family moved a lot when she was growing up. She remembers her growing sense of wonder at the world. Her pleasure in Manitoba summers, riding a sorrel cow pony named June. Plenty of daydreaming, plenty of freedom. In addition to writing, Lynne has worked in adult education and has studied Chinese language and philosophy. She lives with her husband and their two sons in Waterloo, Ontario.